IRISH MYTHS AND LEGENDS

IRISH
MYTHS AND
LEGENDS

Ancient Tales of Gods, Goddesses and Otherworldly Folk

SIRIUS

SIRIUS

This edition published in 2024 by Sirius Publishing, a division of
Arcturus Publishing Limited,
26/27 Bickels Yard, 151–153 Bermondsey Street,
London SE1 3HA

ISBN: 978-1-3988-4445-2
AD012241UK

Printed in China

CONTENTS

INTRODUCTION

'If you would know Ireland – body and soul – you must read its poems and stories.'
W.B. Yeats

Tales as old as time exist in societies across the globe and have, for millennia, moulded the cultural histories of the lands to which they belong. Such is also the case for Ireland, often dubbed 'the Emerald Isle' and dotted with ancient monuments and medieval castles rooted in myth and legend. From trooping fairies and leprechauns to fiery warriors and fearsome giants, myriad fantastical creatures are known to us today because of the stories that have been passed down and preserved by generations of Irish men and women.

Compiled here are a number of enthralling Irish narratives penned by some of the greatest contributors to the nation's literary heritage. Included are James Stephens, Lady Gregory, Patrick Kennedy, Lady Wilde and many more. Within these pages lie tales of honour, heroism and morality that speak to the essence of Irish identity and highlight a culture that lies with the spirit of its people.

This captivating collection showcases retellings of timeless fables such as Patrick Kennedy's 'The Twelve Wild Geese' as well as long-established Celtic sagas such 'The Birth of Fin MacCumhail'. Also included is Lady Wilde's 'The Leprehaun', Joseph Jacobs' 'Conall

Yellowclaw', and Lady Gregory's 'The Fate of the Children of Lir' taken from their popular published works *Ancient Legends of Ireland, Celtic Fairy Tales* and *Of Gods and Fighting Men,* respectively. Sweeping landscapes, unexpected encounters and otherworldly beings come to life in these vivid narratives that underscore the enduring legacy of the stories of the past.

Embark on an adventure with this fantastic assortment of myths and legends abounding with gods, kings, saviours and spirits. As entertaining as they are insightful, the tales inside will transport readers to ancient landmarks and provide a glimpse into the culture and wisdom that has shaped Ireland through the ages.

A NOTE ON NAMES

The stories in this book have come from a collection of books by acclaimed writers who contributed greatly to Irish literature in the nineteenth and twentieth centuries. As with most tales preserved through oral retellings and gathered separately from different groups of people, there exists a variation of spellings for Ireland's magical people and otherworldly creatures. Below are some examples of the names present within these pages.

The great Irish warrior known as Lug Longhand in Jeremiah Curtin's 'Cucúlin' is also known as Lui Longhand and Lui Lavada in 'Balor on Tory Island'.

Often spelt as 'Leprechauns', Lady Wilde adopts the spelling 'Leprehauns' while Joseph Jacobs uses 'Lepracauns'.

The mighty demigod Finn McCool also has many alternative spellings such as Fin, Finn and Fionn and MacCool, McCool, mac Cumhaill, and MacCumhail.

Ultimately, the spellings and names may differ and references may change but the characters that appear in many of these stories are the same as elsewhere in the book and the greater realm of Irish myth and legend.

THE FIELD OF BOLIAUNS

By Joseph Jacobs

One fine day in harvest – it was indeed Lady-day in harvest, that everybody knows to be one of the greatest holidays in the year – Tom Fitzpatrick was taking a ramble through the ground, and went along the sunny side of a hedge; when all of a sudden he heard a clacking sort of noise a little before him in the hedge. 'Dear me,' said Tom, 'but isn't it surprising to hear the stonechatters singing so late in the season?' So Tom stole on, going on the tops of his toes to try if he could get a sight of what was making the noise, to see if he was right in his guess. The noise stopped; but as Tom looked sharply through the bushes, what should he see in a nook of the hedge but a brown pitcher, that might hold about a gallon and a half of liquor; and by-and-by a little wee teeny tiny bit of an old man, with a little *motty* of a cocked hat stuck upon the top of his head, a deeshy daushy leather apron hanging before him, pulled out a little wooden stool, and stood up upon it, and dipped a little piggin into the pitcher, and took out the full of it, and put it beside the stool, and then sat down under the pitcher, and began to work at putting a heel-piece on a bit of a

11

brogue just fit for himself. 'Well, by the powers,' said Tom to himself, 'I often heard tell of the Lepracauns, and, to tell God's truth, I never rightly believed in them – but here's one of them in real earnest. If I go knowingly to work, I'm a made man. They say a body must never take their eyes off them, or they'll escape.'

Tom now stole on a little further, with his eye fixed on the little man just as a cat does with a mouse. So when he got up quite close to him, 'God bless your work, neighbour,' said Tom.

The little man raised up his head, and 'Thank you kindly,' said he.

'I wonder you'd be working on the holiday!' said Tom.

'That's my own business, not yours,' was the reply.

'Well, maybe you'd be civil enough to tell *us* what you've got in the pitcher there?' said Tom.

'That I will, with pleasure,' said he; 'it's good beer.'

'Beer!' said Tom. 'Thunder and fire! where did you get it?'

'Where did I get it, is it? Why, I made it. And what do you think I made it of?'

'Devil a one of me knows,' said Tom; 'but of malt, I suppose, what else?'

'There you're out. I made it of heath.'

'Of heath!' said Tom, bursting out laughing; 'sure you don't think me to be such a fool as to believe that?'

'Do as you please,' said he, 'but what I tell you is the truth. Did you never hear tell of the Danes?'

'Well, what about *them*?' said Tom.

'Why, all the about them there is, is that when they were here they taught us to make beer out of the heath, and the secret's in my family ever since.'

'Will you give a body a taste of your beer?' said Tom.

'I'll tell you what it is, young man, it would be fitter for you to be looking after your father's property than to be bothering decent quiet people with your foolish questions. There now, while you're idling away your time here, there's the cows have broke into the oats, and are knocking the corn all about.'

Tom was taken so by surprise with this that he was just on the very point of turning round when he recollected himself; so, afraid that the like might happen again, he made a grab at the Lepracaun, and caught him up in his hand; but in his hurry he overset the pitcher, and spilt all the beer, so that he could not get a taste of it to tell what sort it was. He then swore that he would kill him if he did not show him where his money was. Tom looked so wicked and so bloody-minded that the little man was quite frightened; so says he, 'Come along with me a couple of fields off, and I'll show you a crock of gold.'

So they went, and Tom held the Lepracaun fast in his hand, and never took his eyes from off him, though they had to cross hedges and ditches, and a crooked bit of bog, till at last they came to a great field all full of boliauns, and the Lepracaun pointed to a big boliaun, and says he, 'Dig under that boliaun, and you'll get the great crock all full of guineas.'

Tom in his hurry had never thought of bringing a spade with him, so he made up his mind to run home and fetch one; and that he might know the place again he took off one of his red garters, and tied it round the boliaun.

Then he said to the Lepracaun, 'Swear ye'll not take that garter away from that boliaun.' And the Lepracaun swore right away not to touch it.

'I suppose,' said the Lepracaun, very civilly, 'you have no further occasion for me?'

'No,' says Tom; 'you may go away now, if you please, and God speed you, and may good luck attend you wherever you go.'

'Well, good-bye to you, Tom Fitzpatrick,' said the Lepracaun; 'and much good may it do you when you get it.'

So Tom ran for dear life, till he came home and got a spade, and then away with him, as hard as he could go, back to the field of boliauns; but when he got there, lo and behold! not a boliaun in the field but had a red garter, the very model of his own, tied about it; and as to digging up the whole field, that was all nonsense, for there were more than forty good Irish acres in it. So Tom came home again with his spade on his shoulder, a little cooler than he went, and many's the hearty curse he gave the Lepracaun every time he thought of the neat turn he had served him.

CONALL YELLOWCLAW

By Joseph Jacobs

Conall Yellowclaw was a sturdy tenant in Erin: he had three sons. There was at that time a king over every fifth of Erin. It fell out for the children of the king that was near Conall, that they themselves and the children of Conall came to blows. The children of Conall got the upper hand, and they killed the king's big son. The king sent a message for Conall, and he said to him – 'Oh, Conall! what made your sons go to spring on my sons till my big son was killed by your children? but I see that though I follow you revengefully, I shall not be much better for it, and I will now set a thing before you, and if you will do it, I will not follow you with revenge. If you and your sons will get me the brown horse of the king of Lochlann, you shall get the souls of your sons.'

'Why,' said Conall, 'should not I do the pleasure of the king, though there should be no souls of my sons in dread at all. Hard is the matter you require of me, but I will lose my own life, and the life of my sons, or else I will do the pleasure of the king.'

After these words Conall left the king, and he went home: when

he got home he was under much trouble and perplexity. When he went to lie down he told his wife the thing the king had set before him. His wife took much sorrow that he was obliged to part from herself, while she knew not if she should see him more.

'Oh, Conall,' said she, 'why didst not thou let the king do his own pleasure to thy sons, rather than be going now, while I know not if ever I shall see thee more?'

When he rose on the morrow, he set himself and his three sons in order, and they took their journey towards Lochlann, and they made no stop but tore through ocean till they reached it. When they reached Lochlann they did not know what they should do. Said the old man to his sons, 'Stop ye, and we will seek out the house of the king's miller.'

When they went into the house of the king's miller, the man asked them to stop there for the night. Conall told the miller that his own children and the children of his king had fallen out, and that his children had killed the king's son, and there was nothing that would please the king but that he should get the brown horse of the king of Lochlann.

'If you will do me a kindness, and will put me in a way to get him, for certain I will pay ye for it.'

'The thing is silly that you are come to seek,' said the miller; 'for the king has laid his mind on him so greatly that you will not get him in any way unless you steal him; but if you can make out a way, I will keep it secret.'

'This is what I am thinking,' said Conall, 'since you are working every day for the king, you and your gillies could put myself and my sons into five sacks of bran.'

'The plan that has come into your head is not bad,' said the miller.

The miller spoke to his gillies, and he said to them to do this, and they put them in five sacks. The king's gillies came to seek the bran, and they took the five sacks with them, and they emptied them before the horses. The servants locked the door, and they went away.

When they rose to lay hand on the brown horse, said Conall, 'You shall not do that. It is hard to get out of this; let us make for ourselves five hiding holes, so that if they hear us we may go and hide.' They made the holes, then they laid hands on the horse. The horse was pretty well unbroken, and he set to making a terrible noise through the stable. The king heard the noise. 'It must be my brown horse,' said he to his gillies; 'find out what is wrong with him.'

The servants went out, and when Conall and his sons saw them coming they went into the hiding holes. The servants looked amongst the horses, and they did not find anything wrong; and they returned and they told this to the king, and the king said to them that if nothing was wrong they should go to their places of rest. When the gillies had time to be gone, Conall and his sons laid their hands again on the horse. If the noise was great that he made before, the noise he made now was seven times greater. The king sent a message for his gillies again, and said for certain there was something troubling the brown horse. 'Go and look well about him.' The servants went out, and they went to their hiding holes. The servants rummaged well, and did not find a thing. They returned and they told this.

'That is marvellous for me,' said the king: 'go you to lie down again, and if I notice it again I will go out myself.'

When Conall and his sons perceived that the gillies were gone, they laid hands again on the horse, and one of them caught him, and

if the noise that the horse made on the two former times was great, he made more this time.

'Be this from me,' said the king; 'it must be that some one is troubling my brown horse.' He sounded the bell hastily, and when his waiting-man came to him, he said to him to let the stable gillies know that something was wrong with the horse. The gillies came, and the king went with them. When Conall and his sons perceived the company coming they went to the hiding holes.

The king was a wary man, and he saw where the horses were making a noise.

'Be wary,' said the king, 'there are men within the stable, let us get at them somehow.'

The king followed the tracks of the men, and he found them. Every one knew Conall, for he was a valued tenant of the king of Erin, and when the king brought them up out of the holes he said, 'Oh, Conall, is it you that are here?'

'I am, O king, without question, and necessity made me come. I am under thy pardon, and under thine honour, and under thy grace.' He told how it happened to him, and that he had to get the brown horse for the king of Erin, or that his sons were to be put to death. 'I knew that I should not get him by asking, and I was going to steal him.'

'Yes, Conall, it is well enough, but come in,' said the king. He desired his look-out men to set a watch on the sons of Conall, and to give them meat. And a double watch was set that night on the sons of Conall.

'Now, O Conall,' said the king, 'were you ever in a harder place than to be seeing your lot of sons hanged tomorrow? But you set it to my goodness and to my grace, and say that it was necessity brought it on you, so I must not hang you. Tell me any case in which you were as hard as this, and if you tell that, you shall get the soul of your youngest son.'

'I will tell a case as hard in which I was,' said Conall. 'I was once a young lad, and my father had much land, and he had parks of year-old cows, and one of them had just calved, and my father told me to bring her home. I found the cow, and took her with us. There fell a shower of snow. We went into the herd's bothy, and we took the cow and the calf in with us, and we were letting the shower pass from us. Who should come in but one cat and ten, and one great one-eyed fox-coloured cat as head bard over them. When they came in, in very deed I myself had no liking for their company. "Strike up with you," said the head bard, "why should we be still? and sing a cronan to Conall Yellowclaw." I was amazed that my name was known to the cats themselves. When they had sung the cronan, said the head bard, "Now, O Conall, pay the reward of the cronan that the cats have sung to thee." "Well then," said I myself, "I have no reward whatsoever for you, unless you should go down and take that calf." No sooner said I the word than the two cats and ten went down to attack the calf, and in very deed, he did not last them long. "Play up with you, why should you be silent? Make a cronan to Conall Yellowclaw," said the head bard. Certainly I had no liking at all for the cronan, but up came the one cat and ten, and if they did not sing me a cronan then and there! "Pay them now their reward," said the great fox-coloured cat. "I am tired myself of yourselves and your rewards," said I. "I have no reward for you unless you take that cow down there."

They betook themselves to the cow, and indeed she did not last them long.

"'Why will you be silent? Go up and sing a cronan to Conall Yellowclaw," said the head bard. And surely, oh king, I had no care for them or for their cronan, for I began to see that they were not good comrades. When they had sung me the cronan they betook themselves down where the head bard was. "Pay now their reward," said the head bard; and for sure, oh king, I had no reward for them; and I said to them, "I have no reward for you." And surely, oh king, there was caterwauling between them. So I leapt out at a turf window that was at the back of the house. I took myself off as hard as I might into the wood. I was swift enough and strong at that time; and when I felt the rustling toirm of the cats after me I climbed into as high a tree as I saw in the place, and one that was close in the top; and I hid myself as well as I might. The cats began to search for me through the wood, and they could not find me; and when they were tired, each one said to the other that they would turn back. "But," said the one-eyed fox-coloured cat that was commander-in-chief over them, "you saw him not with your two eyes, and though I have but one eye, there's the rascal up in the tree." When he had said that, one of them went up in the tree, and as he was coming where I was, I drew a weapon that I had and I killed him. "Be this from me!" said the one-eyed one – "I must not be losing my company thus; gather round the root of the tree and dig about it, and let down that villain to earth." On this they gathered about the tree, and they dug about the root, and the first branching root that they cut, she gave a shiver to fall, and I myself gave a shout, and it was not to be wondered at.

'There was in the neighbourhood of the wood a priest, and he had ten men with him delving, and he said, "There is a shout of a man in extremity and I must not be without replying to it." And the wisest of the men said, "Let it alone till we hear it again." The cats began again digging wildly, and they broke the next root; and I myself gave the next shout, and in very deed it was not a weak one. "Certainly," said the priest, "it is a man in extremity – let us move." They set themselves in order for moving. And the cats arose on the tree, and they broke the third root, and the tree fell on her elbow. Then I gave the third shout. The stalwart men hastened, and when they saw how the cats served the tree, they began at them with the spades; and they themselves and the cats began at each other, till the cats ran away. And surely, oh king, I did not move till I saw the last one of them off. And then I came home. And there's the hardest case in which I ever was; and it seems to me that tearing by the cats were harder than hanging tomorrow by the king of Lochlann.'

'Och! Conall,' said the king, 'you are full of words. You have freed the soul of your son with your tale; and if you tell me a harder case than that you will get your second youngest son, and then you will have two sons.'

'Well then,' said Conall, 'on condition that thou dost that, I will tell thee how I was once in a harder case than to be in thy power in prison tonight.'

'Let's hear,' said the king.

'I was then,' said Conall, 'quite a young lad, and I went out hunting, and my father's land was beside the sea, and it was rough with rocks, caves, and rifts. When I was going on the top of the shore, I saw as if there were a smoke coming up between two rocks,

and I began to look what might be the meaning of the smoke coming up there. When I was looking, what should I do but fall; and the place was so full of heather, that neither bone nor skin was broken. I knew not how I should get out of this. I was not looking before me, but I kept looking overhead the way I came – and thinking that the day would never come that I could get up there. It was terrible for me to be there till I should die. I heard a great clattering coming, and what was there but a great giant and two dozen of goats with him, and a buck at their head. And when the giant had tied the goats, he came up and he said to me, "Hao O! Conall, it's long since my knife has been rusting in my pouch waiting for thy tender flesh." "Och!" said I, "it's not much you will be bettered by me, though you should tear me asunder; I will make but one meal for you. But I see that you are one-eyed. I am a good leech, and I will give you the sight of the other eye." The giant went and he drew the great caldron on the site of the fire. I myself was telling him how he should heat the water, so that I should give its sight to the other eye. I got heather and I made a rubber of it, and I set him upright in the caldron. I began at the eye that was well, pretending to him that I would give its sight to the other one, till I left them as bad as each other; and surely it was easier to spoil the one that was well than to give sight to the other.

'When he saw that he could not see a glimpse, and when I myself said to him that I would get out in spite of him, he gave a spring out of the water, and he stood in the mouth of the cave, and he said that he would have revenge for the sight of his eye. I had but to stay there crouched the length of the night, holding in my breath in such a way that he might not find out where I was.

'When he felt the birds calling in the morning, and knew that the day was, he said – "Art thou sleeping? Awake and let out my lot of goats." I killed the buck. He cried, "I do believe that thou art killing my buck."

'"I am not," said I, "but the ropes are so tight that I take long to loose them." I let out one of the goats, and there he was caressing her, and he said to her, "There thou art thou shaggy, hairy white goat; and thou seest me, but I see thee not." I kept letting them out by the way of one and one, as I flayed the buck, and before the last one was out I had him flayed bag-wise. Then I went and I put my legs in place of his legs, and my hands in place of his forelegs, and my head in place of his head, and the horns on top of my head, so that the brute might think that it was the buck. I went out. When I was going out the giant laid his hand on me, and he said, "There thou art, thou pretty buck; thou seest me, but I see thee not." When I myself got out, and I saw the world about me, surely, oh, king! joy was on me. When I was out and had shaken the skin off me, I said to the brute, "I am out now in spite of you."

'"Aha!" said he, "hast thou done this to me. Since thou wert so stalwart that thou hast got out, I will give thee a ring that I have here; keep the ring, and it will do thee good."

'"I will not take the ring from you," said I, "but throw it, and I will take it with me." He threw the ring on the flat ground, I went myself and I lifted the ring, and I put it on my finger. When he said me then, "Is the ring fitting thee?" I said to him, "It is." Then he said, "Where art thou, ring?" And the ring said, "I am here." The brute went and went towards where the ring was speaking, and now I saw that I was in a harder case than ever I was. I drew a dirk. I cut the

finger from off me, and I threw it from me as far as I could out on the loch, and there was a great depth in the place. He shouted, "Where art thou, ring?" And the ring said, "I am here," though it was on the bed of ocean. He gave a spring after the ring, and out he went in the sea. And I was as pleased then when I saw him drowning, as though you should grant my own life and the life of my two sons with me, and not lay any more trouble on me.

'When the giant was drowned I went in, and I took with me all he had of gold and silver, and I went home, and surely great joy was on my people when I arrived. And as a sign now look, the finger is off me.'

'Yes, indeed, Conall, you are wordy and wise,' said the king. 'I see the finger is off you. You have freed your two sons, but tell me a case in which you ever were that is harder than to be looking on your son being hanged tomorrow, and you shall get the soul of your eldest son.'

'Then went my father,' said Conall, 'and he got me a wife, and I was married. I went to hunt. I was going beside the sea, and I saw an island over in the midst of the loch, and I came there where a boat was with a rope before her, and a rope behind her, and many precious things within her. I looked myself on the boat to see how I might get part of them. I put in the one foot, and the other foot was on the ground, and when I raised my head what was it but the boat over in the middle of the loch, and she never stopped till she reached the island. When I went out of the boat the boat returned where she was before. I did not know now what I should do. The place was without meat or clothing, without the appearance of a house on it. I came out on the top of a hill. Then I came to a glen; I saw in it, at the bottom of a hollow, a woman with a child, and the child was naked on her knee, and she had a knife in her hand. She tried to put the knife to the throat of the babe, and the babe began to laugh in her face, and she began to cry, and she threw the knife behind her. I thought to myself that I was near my foe and far from my friends, and I called to the woman, "What are you doing here?" And she said to me, "What brought you here?" I told her myself word upon word how I came. "Well then," said she, "it was so I came also." She showed me to the place where I should come in where she was. I went in, and I said to her, "What was the matter that you were putting the knife on the neck of the child?" "It is that he must be cooked for the giant who is here, or else no more of my world will be before me." Just then we could be hearing the footsteps of the giant, "What shall I do? what shall I do?" cried the woman. I went to the caldron, and by luck it was not hot, so in it I got just as the brute came in. "Hast thou boiled that youngster for me?" he cried. "He's not done yet," said she, and I cried out from the caldron, "Mammy, mammy, it's boiling I am." Then the giant laughed out HAI, HAW, HOGARAICH, and heaped on wood under the caldron.

'And now I was sure I would scald before I could get out of that. As fortune favoured me, the brute slept beside the caldron. There I was scalded by the bottom of the caldron. When she perceived that he was asleep, she set her mouth quietly to the hole that was in the lid, and she said to me "was I alive?" I said I was. I put up my head, and the hole in the lid was so large, that my head went through easily. Everything was coming easily with me till I began to bring up my hips. I left the skin of my hips behind me, but I came out. When I got out of the caldron I knew not what to do; and she said to me that there was no weapon that would kill him but his own weapon. I began to draw his spear and every breath that he drew I thought I would be down his throat, and when his breath came out I was back again just as far. But with every ill that befell me I got the spear loosed from him. Then I was as one under a bundle of straw in a great wind for I could not manage the spear. And it was fearful to look on the brute, who had but one eye in the midst of his face; and it was not agreeable for the like of me to attack him. I drew the dart as best I could, and I set it in his eye. When he felt this he gave his head a lift, and he struck the other end of the dart on the top of the cave, and it went through to the back of his head. And he fell cold dead where he was; and you may be sure, oh king, that joy was on me. I myself and the woman went out on clear ground, and we passed the night there. I went and got the boat with which I came, and she was no way lightened, and took the woman and the child over on dry land; and I returned home.'

The king of Lochlann's mother was putting on a fire at this time, and listening to Conall telling the tale about the child.

'Is it you,' said she, 'that were there?'

'Well then,' said he, ''twas I.'

'Och! och!' said she, ''twas I that was there, and the king is the child whose life you saved; and it is to you that life thanks should be given.' Then they took great joy.

The king said, 'Oh, Conall, you came through great hardships. And now the brown horse is yours, and his sack full of the most precious things that are in my treasury.'

They lay down that night, and if it was early that Conall rose, it was earlier than that that the queen was on foot making ready. He got the brown horse and his sack full of gold and silver and stones of great price, and then Conall and his three sons went away, and they returned home to the Erin realm of gladness. He left the gold and silver in his house, and he went with the horse to the king. They were good friends evermore. He returned home to his wife, and they set in order a feast; and that was a feast if ever there was one, oh son and brother.

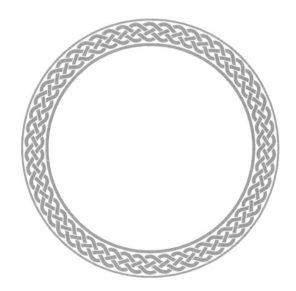

THE TWELVE WILD GEESE

By Patrick Kennedy

There was once a king and queen that lived very happily together, and they had twelve sons and not a single daughter. We are always wishing for what we haven't, and don't care for what we have, and so it was with the queen. One day in winter, when the bawn was covered with snow, she was looking out of the parlour window, and saw there a calf that was just killed by the butcher, and a raven standing near it. 'Oh,' says she, 'if I had only a daughter with her skin as white as that snow, her cheeks as red as that blood, and her hair as black as that raven, I'd give away every one of my twelve sons for her.' The moment she said the word, she got a great fright, and a shiver went through her, and in an instant after, a severe-looking old woman stood before her. 'That was a wicked wish you made,' said she, 'and to punish you it will be granted. You will have such a daughter as you desire, but the very day of her birth you will lose your other children.' She vanished the moment she said the words.

And that very way it turned out. When she expected her delivery, she had her children all in a large room of the palace, with guards all round it, but the very hour her daughter came into the world, the guards inside and outside heard a great whirling and whistling, and the twelve princes were seen flying one after another out through the open window, and away like so many arrows over the woods. Well, the king was in great grief for the loss of his sons, and he would be very enraged with his wife if he only knew that she was so much to blame for it.

Everyone called the little princess Snow-white-and-Rose-red on account of her beautiful complexion. She was the most loving and lovable child that could be seen anywhere. When she was twelve years old she began to be very sad and lonely, and to torment her mother, asking her about her brothers that she thought were dead, for none up to that time ever told her the exact thing that happened to them. The secret was weighing very heavy on the queen's conscience, and as the little girl persevered in her questions, at last she told her. 'Well, mother,' said she, 'it was on my account my poor brothers were changed into wild geese, and are now suffering all sorts of hardship: before the world is a day older, I'll be off to seek them, and try to restore them to their own shapes.'

The king and queen had her well watched, but all was no use. Next night she was getting through the woods that surrounded the palace, and she went on and on that night, and till the evening of next day. She had a few cakes with her, and she got nuts, and *mugoreens* (fruit of the sweet briar), and some sweet crabs, as she went along. At last she came to a nice wooden house just at sunset. There was a fine garden round it, full of the handsomest flowers, and a gate in the hedge. She went in, and saw a table laid out with twelve plates, and twelve knives and forks, and twelve spoons, and there were cakes,

and cold wild fowl, and fruit along with the plates, and there was a good fire, and in another long room there were twelve beds. Well, while she was looking about her she heard the gate opening, and footsteps along the walk, and in came twelve young men, and there was great grief and surprise on all their faces when they laid eyes on her. 'Oh, what misfortune sent you here?' said the eldest. 'For the sake of a girl we were obliged to leave our father's court, and be in the shape of wild geese all day. That's twelve years ago, and we took a solemn oath that we would kill the first young girl that came into our hands. It's a pity to put such an innocent and handsome girl as you are out of the world, but we must keep our oath.' 'But,' said she, 'I'm your only sister, that never knew anything about this till yesterday; and I stole away from our father's and mother's palace last night to find you out and relieve you if I can.' Every one of them clasped his hands, and looked down on the floor, and you could hear a pin fall till the eldest cried out, 'A curse light on our oath! what shall we do?' 'I'll tell you that,' said an old woman that appeared at the instant among them. 'Break your wicked oath, which no one should keep. If you attempted to lay an uncivil finger on her I'd change you into twelve *booliaun buis* (stalks of ragweed), but I wish well to you as well as to her. She is appointed to be your deliverer in this way. She must spin and knit twelve shirts for you out of bog-down, to be gathered by her own hands on the moor just outside of the wood. It will take her five years to do it, and if she once speaks, or laughs, or cries the whole time, you will have to remain wild geese by day till you're called out of the world. So take care of your sister; it is worth your while.' The fairy then vanished, and it was only a strife with the brothers to see who would be first to kiss and hug their sister.

So for three long years the poor young princess was occupied pulling bog-down, spinning it, and knitting it into shirts, and at the end of the three years she had eight made. During all that time, she never spoke a word, nor laughed, nor cried: the last was the hardest to refrain from. One fine day she was sitting in the garden spinning, when in sprung a fine greyhound and bounded up to her, and laid his paws on her shoulder, and licked her forehead and her hair. The next minute a beautiful young prince rode up to the little garden gate, took off his hat, and asked for leave to come in. She gave him a little nod, and in he walked. He made ever so many apologies for intruding, and asked her ever so many questions, but not a word could he get out of her. He loved her so much from the first moment, that he could not leave her till he told her he was king of a country just bordering on the forest, and he begged her to come home with him, and be his wife. She couldn't help loving him as much as he did her, and though she shook her head very often, and was very sorry to leave her brothers, at last she nodded her head, and put her hand in his. She knew well enough that the good fairy and her brothers would be able to find her out. Before she went she brought out a basket holding all her bog-down, and another holding the eight shirts. The attendants took charge of these, and the prince placed her before him on his horse. The only thing that disturbed him while riding along was the displeasure his stepmother would feel at what he had done. However, he was full master at home, and as soon as he arrived he sent for the bishop, got his bride nicely dressed, and the marriage was celebrated, the bride answering by signs. He knew by her manners she was of high birth, and no two could be fonder of each other.

The wicked stepmother did all she could to make mischief, saying she was sure she was only a woodman's daughter; but nothing could disturb the young king's opinion of his wife. In good time the young queen was delivered of a beautiful boy, and the king was so glad he hardly knew what to do for joy. All the grandeur of the christening and the happiness of the parents tormented the bad woman more than I can tell you, and she determined to put a stop to all their comfort. She got a sleeping posset given to the young mother, and while she was thinking and thinking how she could best make away with the child, she saw a wicked-looking wolf in the garden, looking up at her, and licking his chops. She lost no time, but snatched the child from the arms of the sleeping woman, and pitched it out. The beast caught it in his mouth, and was over the garden fence in a minute. The wicked woman then pricked her own fingers, and dabbled the blood round the mouth of the sleeping mother.

Well, the young king was just then coming into the big bawn from hunting, and as soon as he entered the house, she beckoned to him, shed a few crocodile tears, began to cry and wring her hands, and hurried him along the passage to the bedchamber.

Oh, wasn't the poor king frightened when he saw the queen's mouth bloody, and missed his child? It would take two hours to tell you the devilment of the old queen, the confusion and fright, and grief of the young king and queen, the bad opinion he began to feel of his wife, and the struggle she had to keep down her bitter sorrow, and not give way to it by speaking or lamenting. The young king would not allow any one to be called, and ordered his stepmother to give out that the child fell from the mother's arms at the window, and that a wild beast ran off with it. The wicked woman pretended to do so, but she told underhand to everybody she spoke to what the king and herself saw in the bedchamber.

The young queen was the most unhappy woman in the three kingdoms for a long time, between sorrow for her child, and her husband's bad opinion; still she neither spoke nor cried, and she gathered bog-down and went on with the shirts. Often the twelve wild geese would be seen lighting on the trees in the park or on the smooth sod, and looking in at her windows. So she worked on to get the shirts finished, but another year was at an end, and she had the twelfth shirt finished except one arm, when she was obliged to take to her bed, and a beautiful girl was born.

Now the king was on his guard, and he would not let the mother and child be left alone for a minute; but the wicked woman bribed some of the attendants, set others asleep, gave the sleepy posset to the queen, and had a person watching to snatch the child away, and kill it. But what should she see but the same wolf in the garden looking up and licking his chops again? Out went the child, and away with it flew the wolf, and she smeared the sleeping mother's mouth and face with blood, and then roared, and bawled, and cried out to the king and to everybody she met, and the room was filled, and everyone was sure the young queen had just devoured her own babe.

The poor mother thought now her life would leave her. She was in such a state she could neither think nor pray, but she sat like a stone, and worked away at the arm of the twelfth shirt.

The king was for taking her to the house in the wood where he found her, but the stepmother, and the lords of the court, and the judges would not hear of it, and she was condemned to be burned in the big bawn at three o'clock the same day. When the hour drew

near, the king went to the farthest part of his palace, and there was no more unhappy man in his kingdom at that hour.

When the executioners came and led her off, she took the pile of shirts in her arms. There were still a few stitches wanted, and while they were tying her to the stakes she still worked on. At the last stitch she seemed overcome and dropped a tear on her work, but the moment after she sprang up, and shouted out, 'I am innocent; call my husband!' The executioners stayed their hands, except one wicked-disposed creature, who set fire to the faggot next him, and while all were struck in amazement, there was a rushing of wings, and in a moment the twelve wild geese were standing around the pile. Before you could count twelve, she flung a shirt over each bird, and there in the twinkling of an eye were twelve of the finest young men that could be collected out of a thousand. While some were untying their sister, the eldest, taking a strong stake in his hand, struck the busy executioner such a blow that he never needed another.

While they were comforting the young queen, and the king was hurrying to the spot, a fine-looking woman appeared among them holding the babe on one arm and the little prince by the hand. There was nothing but crying for joy, and laughing for joy, and hugging and kissing, and when any one had time to thank the good fairy, who in the shape of a wolf, carried the child away, she was not to be found. Never was such happiness enjoyed in any palace that ever was built, and if the wicked queen and her helpers were not torn by wild horses, they richly deserved it.

THE LEPREHAUN

By Lady Wilde

The Leprehauns are merry, industrious, tricksy little sprites, who do all the shoemaker's work and the tailor's and the cobbler's for the fairy gentry, and are often seen at sunset under the hedge singing and stitching. They know all the secrets of hidden treasure, and if they take a fancy to a person will guide him to the spot in the fairy rath where the pot of gold lies buried. It is believed that a family now living near Castlerea came by their riches in a strange way, all through the good offices of a friendly Leprehaun. And the legend has been handed down through many generations as an established fact.

There was a poor boy once, one of their forefathers, who used to drive his cart of turf daily back and forward, and make what money he could by the sale; but he was a strange boy, very silent and moody, and the people said he was a fairy changeling, for he joined in no sports and scarcely ever spoke to any one, but spent the nights reading all the old bits of books he picked up in his rambles. The one thing he longed for above all others was to get rich, and to be able

to give up the old weary turf cart, and live in peace and quietness all alone, with nothing but books round him, in a beautiful house and garden all by himself.

Now he had read in the old books how the Leprehauns knew all the secret places where gold lay hid, and day by day he watched for a sight of the little cobbler, and listened for the click, click of his hammer as he sat under the hedge mending the shoes.

At last, one evening just as the sun set, he saw a little fellow under a dock leaf, working away, dressed all in green, with a cocked hat on his head. So the boy jumped down from the cart and seized him by the neck.

'Now, you don't stir from this,' he cried, 'till you tell me where to find the hidden gold.'

'Easy now,' said the Leprehaun, 'don't hurt me, and I will tell you all about it. But mind you, I could hurt you if I chose, for I have the power; but I won't do it, for we are cousins once removed. So as we are near relations I'll just be good, and show you the place of the secret gold that none can have or keep except those of fairy blood and race. Come along with me, then, to the old fort of Lipenshaw, for there it lies. But make haste, for when the last red glow of the sun vanishes the gold will disappear also, and you will never find it again.'

'Come off, then,' said the boy, and he carried the Leprehaun into the turf cart, and drove off. And in a second they were at the old fort, and went in through a door made in the stone wall.

'Now, look round,' said the Leprehaun; and the boy saw the whole ground covered with gold pieces, and there were vessels of silver lying about in such plenty that all the riches of all the world seemed gathered there.

'Now take what you want,' said the Leprehaun, 'but hasten, for if that door shuts you will never leave this place as long as you live.'

So the boy gathered up his arms full of gold and silver, and flung them into the cart; and was on his way back for more when the door shut with a clap like thunder, and all the place became dark as night. And he saw no more of the Leprehaun, and had not time even to thank him.

So he thought it best to drive home at once with his treasure, and when he arrived and was all alone by himself he counted his riches, and all the bright yellow gold pieces, enough for a king's ransom.

And he was very wise and told no one; but went off next day to Dublin and put all his treasures into the bank, and found that he was now indeed as rich as a lord.

So he ordered a fine house to be built with spacious gardens, and he had servants and carriages and books to his heart's content. And he gathered all the wise men round him to give him the learning of a gentleman; and he became a great and powerful man in the country, where his memory is still held in high honour, and his descendants are living to this day rich and prosperous; for their wealth has never decreased though they have ever given largely to the poor, and are noted above all things for the friendly heart and the liberal hand.

But the Leprehauns can be bitterly malicious if they are offended, and one should be very cautious in dealing with them, and always treat them with great civility, or they will take revenge and never reveal the secret of the hidden gold.

One day a young lad was out in the fields at work when he saw a little fellow, not the height of his hand, mending shoes under a dock leaf. And he went over, never taking his eyes off him for fear he would vanish away; and when he got quite close he made a grab at the creature, and lifted him up and put him in his pocket.

Then he ran away home as fast as he could, and when he had the Leprehaun safe in the house, he tied him by an iron chain to the hob.

'Now, tell me,' he said, 'where am I to find a pot of gold? Let me know the place or I'll punish you.'

'I know of no pot of gold,' said the Leprehaun; 'but let me go that I may finish mending the shoes.'

'Then I'll make you tell me,' said the lad.

And with that he made down a great fire, and put the little fellow on it and scorched him.

'Oh, take me off, take me off!' cried the Leprehaun, 'and I'll tell you. Just there, under the dock leaf, where you found me, there is a pot of gold. Go; dig and find.'

So the lad was delighted, and ran to the door; but it so happened that his mother was just then coming in with the pail of fresh milk, and in his haste he knocked the pail out of her hand, and all the milk was spilled on the floor.

Then, when the mother saw the Leprehaun, she grew very angry and beat him. 'Go away, you little wretch!' she cried. 'You have overlooked the milk and brought ill-luck.' And she kicked him out of the house.

But the lad ran off to find the dock leaf, though he came back very sorrowful in the evening, for he had dug and dug nearly down to the middle of the earth; but no pot of gold was to be seen.

That same night the husband was coming home from his work, and as he passed the old fort he heard voices and laughter, and one said –

'They are looking for a pot of gold; but they little know that a crock of gold is lying down in the bottom of the old quarry, hid under the stones close by the garden wall. But whoever gets it must go of a dark night at twelve o'clock, and beware of bringing his wife with him.'

So the man hurried home and told his wife he would go that very night, for it was black dark, and she must stay at home and watch for him, and not stir from the house till he came back. Then he went out into the dark night alone.

'Now,' thought the wife, when he was gone, 'if I could only get to the quarry before him I would have the pot of gold all to myself; while if he gets it I shall have nothing.'

And with that she went out and ran like the wind until she reached the quarry, and then she began to creep down very quietly in the black dark. But a great stone was in her path, and she stumbled over it, and fell down and down till she reached the bottom, and there she lay groaning, for her leg was broken by the fall.

Just then her husband came to the edge of the quarry and began to descend. But when he heard the groans he was frightened.

'Cross of Christ about us!' he exclaimed; 'what is that down below? Is it evil, or is it good?'

'Oh, come down, come down and help me!' cried the woman. 'It's your wife is here, and my leg is broken, and I'll die if you don't help me.'

'And is this my pot of gold?' exclaimed the poor man. 'Only my wife with a broken leg lying at the bottom of the quarry.'

And he was at his wits' end to know what to do, for the night was so dark he could not see a hand before him. So he roused up a neighbour, and between them they dragged up the poor woman and carried her home, and laid her on the bed half dead from fright, and it was many a day before she was able to get about as usual; indeed she limped all her life long, so that the people said the curse of the Leprehaun was on her.

But as to the pot of gold, from that day to this not one of the family, father or son, or any belonging to them, ever set eyes on it. However, the little Leprehaun still sits under the dock leaf of the hedge and laughs at them as he mends the shoes with his little hammer – tick tack, tick tack – but they are afraid to touch him, for now they know he can take his revenge.

THE LEGEND OF
BALLYTOWTAS CASTLE

By Lady Wilde

The next tale I shall select is composed in a lighter and more modern spirit. All the usual elements of a fairy tale are to be found in it, but the story is new to the nursery folk, and, if well illustrated, would make a pleasant and novel addition to the rather worn-out legends on which the children of many generations have been hitherto subsisting.

In old times there lived where Ballytowtas Castle now stands a poor man named Towtas. It was in the time when manna fell to the earth with the dew of evening, and Towtas lived by gathering the manna, and thus supported himself, for he was a poor man, and had nothing else.

One day a pedlar came by that way with a fair young daughter.

'Give us a night's lodging,' he said to Towtas, 'for we are weary.'

And Towtas did so.

Next morning, when they were going away, his heart longed for the young girl, and he said to the pedlar, 'Give me your daughter for my wife.'

'How will you support her?' asked the pedlar.

'Better than you can,' answered Towtas, 'for she can never want.'

Then he told him all about the manna; how he went out every morning when it was lying on the ground with the dew, and gathered it, as his father and forefathers had done before him, and lived on it all their lives, so that he had never known want nor any of his people.

Then the girl showed she would like to stay with the young man, and the pedlar consented, and they were married, Towtas and the fair young maiden; and the pedlar left them and went on his way. So years went on, and they were very happy and never wanted; and they had one son, a bright, handsome youth, and as clever as he was comely.

But in due time old Towtas died, and after her husband was buried, the woman went out to gather the manna as she had seen him do, when the dew lay on the ground; but she soon grew tired and said to herself, 'Why should I do this thing every day? I'll just gather now enough to do the week and then I can have rest.'

So she gathered up great heaps of it greedily, and went her way into the house. But the sin of greediness lay on her evermore; and not a bit of manna fell with the dew that evening, nor ever again. And she was poor, and faint with hunger, and had to go out and work in the fields to earn the morsel that kept her and her son alive; and she begged pence from the people as they went into chapel, and this paid for her son's schooling; so he went on with his learning, and no one in the county was like him for beauty and knowledge.

One day he heard the people talking of a great lord that lived up in Dublin, who had a daughter so handsome that her like was never seen; and all the fine young gentlemen were dying about her, but she would take none of them. And he came home to his mother and said, 'I shall go see this great lord's daughter. Maybe the luck will be mine above all the fine young gentlemen that love her.'

'Go along, poor fool,' said the mother, 'how can the poor stand before the rich?'

But he persisted. 'If I die on the road,' he said, 'I'll try it.'

'Wait, then,' she answered, 'till Sunday, and whatever I get I'll give you half of it.' So she gave him half of the pence she gathered at the chapel door, and bid him go in the name of God.

He hadn't gone far when he met a poor man who asked him for a trifle for God's sake. So he gave him something out of his mother's money and went on. Again, another met him, and begged for a trifle to buy food, for the sake of God, and he gave him something also, and then went on.

'Give me a trifle for God's sake,' cried a voice, and he saw a third poor man before him.

'I have nothing left,' said Towtas, 'but a few pence; if I give them, I shall have nothing for food and must die of hunger. But come with me, and whatever I can buy for this I shall share with you.' And as they were going on to the inn he told all his story to the beggar man, and how he wanted to go to Dublin, but had now no money. So they came to the inn, and he called for a loaf and a drink of milk.

'Cut the loaf,' he said to the beggar. 'You are the oldest.'

'I won't,' said the other, for he was ashamed, but Towtas made him. And so the beggar cut the loaf, but though they ate, it never grew

smaller, and though they drank as they liked of the milk, it never grew less. Then Towtas rose up to pay, but when the landlady came and looked, 'How is this?' she said. 'You have eaten nothing. I'll not take your money, poor boy,' but he made her take some; and they left the place, and went on their way together.

'Now,' said the beggar man, 'you have been three times good to me to-day, for thrice I have met you, and you gave me help for the sake of God each time. See, now, I can help also,' and he reached a gold ring to the handsome youth. 'Wherever you place that ring, and wish for it, gold will come – bright gold, so that you can never want while you have it.'

Then Towtas put the ring first in one pocket and then in another, until all his pockets were so heavy with gold that he could scarcely walk; but when he turned to thank the friendly beggar man, he had disappeared.

So, wondering to himself at all his adventures, he went on, until he came at last in sight of the lord's palace, which was beautiful to see; but he would not enter in until he went and bought fine clothes, and made himself as grand as any prince; and then he went boldly up, and they invited him in, for they said, 'Surely he is a king's son.' And when dinner-hour came the lord's daughter linked her arm with Towtas, and smiled on him.

And he drank of the rich wine, and was mad with love; but at last the wine overcame him, and the servants had to carry him to his bed; and in going into his room he dropped the ring from his finger, but knew it not.

Now, in the morning, the lord's daughter came by, and cast her eyes upon the door of his chamber, and there close by it was the ring she had seen him wear.

'Ah,' she said, 'I'll tease him now about his ring.' And she put it in her box, and wished that she were as rich as a king's daughter, that so the king's son might marry her; and, behold, the box filled up with gold, so that she could not shut it; and she put it from her into another box, and that filled also; and then she was frightened at the ring, and put it at last in her pocket as the safest place.

But when Towtas awoke and missed the ring, his heart was grieved.

'Now, indeed,' he said, 'my luck is gone.'

And he inquired of all the servants, and then of the lord's daughter, and she laughed, by which he knew she had it; but no coaxing would get it from her, so when all was useless he went away, and set out again to reach his old home.

And he was very mournful and threw himself down on the ferns near an old fort, waiting till night came on, for he feared to go home in the daylight lest the people should laugh at him for his folly. And about dusk three cats came out of the fort talking to each other.

'How long our cook is away,' said one.

'What can have happened to him?' said another.

And as they were grumbling a fourth cat came up.

'What delayed you?' they all asked angrily.

Then he told his story – how he had met Towtas and given him the ring. 'And I just went,' he said, 'to the lord's palace to see how the young man behaved; and I was leaping over the dinner table when the lord's knife struck my tail and three drops of blood fell upon his plate, but he

never saw it and swallowed them with his meat. So now he has three kittens inside him and is dying of agony, and can never be cured until he drinks three draughts of the water of the well of Ballytowtas.'

So when young Towtas heard the cats talk he sprang up and went and told his mother to give him three bottles full of the water of the Towtas well, and he would go to the lord disguised as a doctor and cure him.

So off he went to Dublin. And all the doctors in Ireland were round the lord, but none of them could tell what ailed him, or how to cure him. Then Towtas came in and said, 'I will cure him.' So they gave him entertainment and lodging, and when he was refreshed he gave of the well water three draughts to his lordship, when out jumped the three kittens. And there was great rejoicing, and they treated Towtas like a prince. But all the same he could not get the ring from the lord's daughter, so he set off home again quite disheartened, and thought to himself, 'If I could only meet the man again that gave me the ring who knows what luck I might have?' And he sat down to rest in a wood, and saw there not far off three boys fighting under an oak-tree.

'Shame on ye to fight so,' he said to them. 'What is the fight about?'

Then they told him. 'Our father,' they said, 'before he died, buried under this oak-tree a ring by which you can be in any place in two minutes if you only wish it; a goblet that is always full when standing, and empty only when on its side; and a harp that plays any tune of itself that you name or wish for.'

'I want to divide the things,' said the youngest boy, 'and let us all go and seek our fortunes as we can.'

'But I have a right to the whole,' said the eldest.

And they went on fighting, till at length Towtas said –

'I'll tell you how to settle the matter. All of you be here tomorrow, and I'll think over the matter tonight, and I engage you will have nothing more to quarrel about when you come in the morning.'

So the boys promised to keep good friends till they met in the morning, and went away.

When Towtas saw them clear off, he dug up the ring, the goblet, and the harp, and now said he, 'I'm all right, and they won't have anything to fight about in the morning.'

Off he set back again to the lord's castle with the ring, the goblet, and the harp; but he soon bethought himself of the powers of the ring, and in two minutes he was in the great hall where all the lords and ladies were just sitting down to dinner; and the harp played the sweetest music, and they all listened in delight; and he drank out of the goblet which was never empty, and then, when his head began to grow a little light, 'It is enough,' he said; and putting his arm round the waist of the lord's daughter, he took his harp and goblet in the other hand, and murmuring – 'I wish we were at the old fort by the side of the wood' – in two minutes they were both at the desired spot. But his head was heavy with the wine, and he laid down the harp beside him and fell asleep. And when she saw him asleep she took the ring off his finger, and the harp and the goblet from the ground and was back home in her father's castle before two minutes had passed by.

When Towtas awoke and found his prize gone, and all his treasures beside, he was like one mad; and roamed about the country till he came by an orchard, where he saw a tree covered with bright, rosy apples. Being hungry and thirsty, he plucked one and ate it, but no

sooner had he done so than horns began to sprout from his forehead, and grew larger and longer till he knew he looked like a goat, and all he could do, they would not come off. Now, indeed, he was driven out of his mind, and thought how all the neighbours would laugh at him; and as he raged and roared with shame, he spied another tree with apples, still brighter, of ruddy gold.

'If I were to have fifty pairs of horns I must have one of those,' he said; and seizing one, he had no sooner tasted it than the horns fell off, and he felt that he was looking stronger and handsomer than ever.

'Now, I have her at last,' he exclaimed. 'I'll put horns on them all, and will never take them off until they give her to me as my bride before the whole Court.'

Without further delay he set off to the lord's palace, carrying with him as many of the apples as he could bring off the two trees. And when they saw the beauty of the fruit they longed for it; and he gave to them all, so that at last there was not a head to be seen without horns in the whole dining-hall. Then they cried out and prayed to have the horns taken off, but Towtas said –

'No; there they shall be till I have the lord's daughter given to me for my bride, and my two rings, my goblet, and my harp all restored to me.'

And this was done before the face of all the lords and ladies; and his treasures were restored to him; and the lord placed his daughter's hand in the hand of Towtas, saying –

'Take her; she is your wife; only free me from the horns.' Then Towtas brought forth the golden apples; and they all ate, and the horns fell off; and he took his bride and his treasures, and carried them off home, where he built the Castle of Ballytowtas, in the place where stood his father's hut, and enclosed the well within the walls. And when he had filled his treasure-room with gold, so that no man could count his riches, he buried his fairy treasures deep in the ground, where no man knew, and no man has ever yet been able to find them until this day.

THE FATE OF THE CHILDREN OF LIR

By Lady Gregory

Now at the time when the Tuatha de Danaan chose a king for themselves after the battle of Tailltin, and Lir heard the kingship was given to Bodb Dearg, it did not please him, and he left the gathering without leave and with no word to any one; for he thought it was he himself had a right to be made king. But if he went away himself, Bodb was given the kingship none the less, for not one of the five begrudged it to him but only Lir. And it is what they determined, to follow after Lir, and to burn down his house, and to attack himself with spear and sword, on account of his not giving obedience to the king they had chosen. 'We will not do that,' said Bodb Dearg, 'for that man would defend any place he is in; and besides that,' he said, 'I am none the less king over the Tuatha de Danaan, although he does not submit to me.'

All went on like that for a good while, but at last a great misfortune came on Lir, for his wife died from him after a sickness of three nights. And that came very hard on Lir, and there was heaviness on his mind after her. And there was great talk of the death of that woman in her own time.

And the news of it was told all through Ireland, and it came to the house of Bodb, and the best of the Men of Dea were with him at that time. And Bodb said: 'If Lir had a mind for it, my help and my friendship would be good for him now, since his wife is not living to him. For I have here with me the three young girls of the best shape, and the best appearance, and the best name in all Ireland, Aobh, Aoife, and Ailbhe, the three daughters of Oilell of Aran, my own three nurselings.' The Men of Dea said then it was a good thought he had, and that what he said was true.

Messages and messengers were sent then from Bodb Dearg to the place Lir was, to say that if he had a mind to join with the Son of the Dagda and to acknowledge his lordship, he would give him a foster-child of his foster-children. And Lir thought well of the offer, and he set out on the morrow with fifty chariots from Sidhe Fionnachaidh; and he went by every short way till he came to Bodb's dwelling-place at Loch Dearg, and there was a welcome before him there, and all the people were merry and pleasant before him, and he and his people got good attendance that night.

And the three daughters of Oilell of Aran were sitting on the one seat with Bodb Dearg's wife, the queen of the Tuatha de Danaan, that was their foster-mother. And Bodb said: 'You may have your choice of the three young girls, Lir.' 'I cannot say,' said Lir, 'which one of them is my choice, but whichever of them is the eldest, she is the noblest, and it is best for me to take her.' 'If that is so,' said Bodb, 'it is Aobh is the eldest, and she will be given to you, if it is your wish.' 'It is my wish,' he said. And he took Aobh for

his wife that night, and he stopped there for a fortnight, and then he brought her away to his own house, till he would make a great wedding-feast.

And in the course of time Aobh brought forth two children, a daughter and a son, Fionnuala and Aodh their names were. And after a while she was brought to bed again, and this time she gave birth to two sons, and they called them Fiachra and Conn. And she herself died at their birth. And that weighed very heavy on Lir, and only for the way his mind was set on his four children he would have gone near to die of grief.

The news came to Bodb Dearg's place, and all the people gave out three loud, high cries, keening their nursling. And after they had keened her it is what Bodb Dearg said: 'It is a fret to us our daughter to have died, for her own sake and for the sake of the good man we gave her to, for we are thankful for his friendship and his faithfulness. However,' he said, 'our friendship with one another will not be broken, for I will give him for a wife her sister Aoife.'

When Lir heard that, he came for the girl and married her, and brought her home to his house. And there was honour and affection with Aoife for her sister's children; and indeed no person at all could see those four children without giving them the heart's love.

And Bodb Dearg used often to be going to Lir's house for the sake of those children; and he used to bring them to his own place for a good length of time, and then he would let them go back to their own place again. And the Men of Dea were at that time using the Feast of Age in every hill of the Sidhe in turn; and when they came to Lir's hill those four children were their joy and delight, for the beauty of their appearance; and it is where they used to sleep, in beds in sight of their father Lir. And he used to rise up at the break of every morning, and to lie down among his children.

But it is what came of all this, that a fire of jealousy was kindled in Aoife, and she got to have a dislike and a hatred of her sister's children.

Then she let on to have a sickness, that lasted through nearly the length of a year. And the end of that time she did a deed of jealousy and cruel treachery against the children of Lir.

And one day she got her chariot yoked, and she took the four children in it, and they went forward towards the house of Bodb Dearg; but Fionnuala had no mind to go with her, for she knew by her she had some plan for their death or their destruction, and she had seen in a dream that there was treachery against them in Aoife's mind. But all the same she was not able to escape from what was before her.

And when they were on their way Aoife said to her people: 'Let you kill now,' she said, 'the four children of Lir, for whose sake their father has given up my love, and I will give you your own choice of a reward out of all the good things of the world.' 'We will not do that indeed,' said they; 'and it is a bad deed you have thought of, and harm will come to you out of it.'

And when they would not do as she bade them, she took out a sword herself to put an end to the children with; but she being a woman and with no good courage, and with no great strength in her mind, she was not able to do it.

They went on then west to Loch Dairbhreach, the Lake of the Oaks, and the horses were stopped there. And Aoife bade the children of Lir to go out and bathe in the lake, and they did as she bade them. And as soon as Aoife saw them out in the lake she struck

them with a Druid rod, and put on them the shape of four swans, white and beautiful. And it is what she said: 'Out with you, children of the king, your luck is taken away from you for ever; it is sorrowful the story will be to your friends; it is with flocks of birds your cries will be heard for ever.'

And Fionnuala said: 'Witch, we know now what your name is, you have struck us down with no hope of relief; but although you put us from wave to wave, there are times when we will touch the land. We shall get help when we are seen; help, and all that is best for us; even though we have to sleep upon the lake, it is our minds will be going abroad early.'

And then the four children of Lir turned towards Aoife, and it is what Fionnuala said: 'It is a bad deed you have done, Aoife, and it is a bad fulfilling of friendship, you to destroy us without cause; and vengeance for it will come upon you, and you will fall in satisfaction for it, for your power for our destruction is not greater than the power of our friends to avenge it on you; and put some bounds now,' she said, 'to the time this enchantment is to stop on us.' 'I will do that,' said Aoife, 'and it is worse for you to have asked it of me. And the bounds I set to your time are this, till the Woman from the South and the Man from the North will come together. And since you ask to hear it of me,' she said, 'no friends and no power that you have will be able to bring you out of these shapes you are in through the length of your lives, until you have been three hundred years on Loch Dairbhreach, and three hundred years on Sruth na Maoile between Ireland and Alban, and three hundred years at Irrus Domnann and Inis Gluaire; and these are to be your journeys from this out,' she said.

But then repentance came on Aoife, and she said: 'Since there is no other help for me to give you now, you may keep your own speech; and you will be singing sweet music of the Sidhe, that would put the men of the earth to sleep, and there will be no music in the world equal to it; and your own sense and your own nobility will stay with you, the way it will not weigh so heavy on you to be in the shape of birds. And go away out of my sight now, children of Lir,' she said, 'with your white faces, with your stammering Irish. It is a great curse on tender lads, they to be driven out on the rough wind. Nine hundred years to be on the water, it is a long time for any one to be in pain; it is I put this on you through treachery, it is best for you to do as I tell you now.

'Lir, that got victory with so many a good cast, his heart is a kernel of death in him now; the groaning of the great hero is a sickness to me, though it is I that have well earned his anger.'

And then the horses were caught for Aoife, and the chariot yoked for her, and she went on to the palace of Bodb Dearg, and there was a welcome before her from the chief people of the place. And the son of the Dagda asked her why she did not bring the children of Lir with her. 'I will tell you that,' she said. 'It is because Lir has no liking for you, and he will not trust you with his children, for fear you might keep them from him altogether.'

'I wonder at that,' said Bodb Dearg, 'for those children are dearer to me than my own children.' And he thought in his own mind it was deceit the woman was doing on him, and it is what he did, he sent messengers to the north to Sidhe Fionnachaidh. And Lir asked them what did they come for. 'On the head of your children,' said they. 'Are they not gone to you along with Aoife?' he said. 'They are

not,' said they; 'and Aoife said it was yourself would not let them come.'

It is downhearted and sorrowful Lir was at that news, for he understood well it was Aoife had destroyed or made an end of his children. And early in the morning of the morrow his horses were caught, and he set out on the road to the south-west. And when he was as far as the shore of Loch Dairbhreach, the four children saw the horses coming towards them, and it is what Fionnuala said: 'A welcome to the troop of horses I see coming near to the lake; the people they are bringing are strong, there is sadness on them; it is us they are following, it is for us they are looking; let us move over to the shore, Aodh, Fiachra, and comely Conn. Those that are coming can be no others in the world but only Lir and his household.'

Then Lir came to the edge of the lake, and he took notice of the swans having the voice of living people, and he asked them why was it they had that voice.

'I will tell you that, Lir,' said Fionnuala. 'We are your own four children, that are after being destroyed by your wife, and by the sister of our own mother, through the dint of her jealousy.' 'Is there any way to put you into your own shapes again?' said Lir. 'There is no way,' said Fionnuala, 'for all the men of the world could not help us till we have gone through our time, and that will not be,' she said, 'till the end of nine hundred years.'

When Lir and his people heard that, they gave out three great heavy shouts of grief and sorrow and crying.

'Is there a mind with you,' said Lir, 'to come to us on the land, since you have your own sense and your memory yet?' 'We have not the power,' said Fionnuala, 'to live with any person at all from this time; but we have our own language, the Irish, and we have the power to sing sweet music, and it is enough to satisfy the whole race of men to be listening to that music. And let you stop here to-night,' she said, 'and we will be making music for you.'

So Lir and his people stopped there listening to the music of the swans, and they slept there quietly that night. And Lir rose up early on the morning of the morrow and he made this complaint:

'It is time to go out from this place. I do not sleep though I am in my lying down. To be parted from my dear children, it is that is tormenting my heart.

'It is a bad net I put over you, bringing Aoife, daughter of Oilell of Aran, to the house. I would never have followed that advice if I had known what it would bring upon me.

'O Fionnuala, and comely Conn, O Aodh, O Fiachra of the beautiful arms; it is not ready I am to go away from you, from the border of the harbour where you are.'

Then Lir went on to the palace of Bodb Dearg, and there was a welcome before him there; and he got a reproach from Bodb Dearg for not bringing his children along with him. 'My grief!' said Lir. 'It is not I that would not bring my children along with me; it was Aoife there beyond, your own foster-child and the sister of their mother, that put them in the shape of four white swans on Loch Dairbhreach, in the sight of the whole of the men of Ireland; but they have their sense with them yet, and their reason, and their voice, and their Irish.'

Bodb Dearg gave a great start when he heard that, and he knew what Lir said was true, and he gave a very sharp reproach to Aoife,

and he said: 'This treachery will be worse for yourself in the end, Aoife, than to the children of Lir. And what shape would you yourself think worst of being in?' he said.

'I would think worst of being a witch of the air,' she said. 'It is into that shape I will put you now,' said Bodb. And with that he struck her with a Druid wand, and she was turned into a witch of the air there and then, and she went away on the wind in that shape, and she is in it yet, and will be in it to the end of life and time.

As to Bodb Dearg and the Tuatha de Danaan they came to the shore of Loch Dairbhreach, and they made their camp there to be listening to the music of the swans.

And the Sons of the Gael used to be coming no less than the Men of Dea to hear them from every part of Ireland, for there never was any music or any delight heard in Ireland to compare with that music of the swans. And they used to be telling stories, and to be talking with the men of Ireland every day, and with their teachers and their fellow-pupils and their friends. And every night they used to sing very sweet music of the Sidhe; and every one that heard that music would sleep sound and quiet whatever trouble or long sickness might be on him; for every one that heard the music of the birds, it is happy and contented he would be after it.

These two gatherings now of the Tuatha de Danaan and of the Sons of the Gael stopped there around Loch Dairbhreach through the length of three hundred years. And it is then Fionnuala said to her brothers: 'Do you know,' she said, 'we have spent all we have to spend of our time here, but this one night only.'

And there was great sorrow on the sons of Lir when they heard that, for they thought it the same as to be living people again, to be talking with their friends and their companions on Loch Dairbhreach, in comparison with going on the cold, fretful sea of the Maoil in the north.

And they came early on the morrow to speak with their father and with their foster-father, and they bade them farewell, and Fionnuala made this complaint:

'Farewell to you, Bodb Dearg, the man with whom all knowledge is in pledge. And farewell to our father along with you, Lir of the Hill of the White Field.

'The time is come, as I think, for us to part from you, O pleasant company; my grief it is not on a visit we are going to you.

'From this day out, O friends of our heart, our comrades, it is on the tormented course of the Maoil we will be, without the voice of any person near us.

'Three hundred years there, and three hundred years in the bay of the men of Domnann, it is a pity for the four comely children of Lir, the salt waves of the sea to be their covering by night.

'O three brothers, with the ruddy faces gone from you, let them all leave the lake now, the great troop that loved us, it is sorrowful our parting is.'

After that complaint they took to flight, lightly, airily, till they came to Sruth na Maoile between Ireland and Alban. And that was a grief to the men of Ireland, and they gave out an order no swan was to be killed from that out, whatever chance there might be of killing one, all through Ireland.

It was a bad dwelling-place for the children of Lir they to be on Sruth na Maoile. When they saw the wide coast about them, they were filled with cold and with sorrow, and they thought nothing of

all they had gone through before, in comparison to what they were going through on that sea.

Now one night while they were there a great storm came on them, and it is what Fionnuala said: 'My dear brothers,' she said, 'it is a pity for us not to be making ready for this night, for it is certain the storm will separate us from one another. And let us,' she said, 'settle on some place where we can meet afterwards, if we are driven from one another in the night.'

'Let us settle,' said the others, 'to meet one another at Carraig na Ron, the Rock of the Seals, for we all have knowledge of it.'

And when midnight came, the wind came on them with it, and the noise of the waves increased, and the lightning was flashing, and a rough storm came sweeping down, the way the children of Lir were scattered over the great sea, and the wideness of it set them astray, so that no one of them could know what way the others went. But after that storm a great quiet came on the sea, and Fionnuala was alone on Sruth na Maoile; and when she took notice that her brothers were wanting she was lamenting after them greatly, and she made this complaint:

'It is a pity for me to be alive in the state I am; it is frozen to my sides my wings are; it is little that the wind has not broken my heart in my body, with the loss of Aodh.

'To be three hundred years on Loch Dairbhreach without going into my own shape, it is worse to me the time I am on Sruth na Maoile.

'The three I loved, Och! the three I loved, that slept under the shelter of my feathers; till the dead come back to the living I will see them no more for ever.

'It is a pity I to stay after Fiachra, and after Aodh, and after comely Conn, and with no account of them; my grief I to be here to face every hardship this night.'

She stopped all night there upon the Rock of the Seals until the rising of the sun, looking out over the sea on every side till at last she saw Conn coming to her, his feathers wet through and his head hanging, and her heart gave him a great welcome; and then Fiachra came wet and perished and worn out, and he could not say a word they could understand with the dint of the cold and the hardship he had gone through. And Fionnuala put him under her wings, and she said: 'We would be well off now if Aodh would but come to us.'

It was not long after that, they saw Aodh coming, his head dry and his feathers beautiful, and Fionnuala gave him a great welcome, and she put him in under the feathers of her breast, and Fiachra under her right wing and Conn under her left wing, the way she could put her feathers over them all. 'And Och! my brothers,' she said, 'this was a bad night to us, and it is many of its like are before us from this out.'

They stayed there a long time after that, suffering cold and misery on the Maoil, till at last a night came on them they had never known the like of before, for frost and snow and wind and cold. And they were crying and lamenting the hardship of their life, and the cold of the night and the greatness of the snow and the hardness of the wind. And after they had suffered cold to the end of a year, a worse night again came on them, in the middle of winter. And they were on Carraig na Ron, and the water froze about them, and as they rested on the rock, their feet and their wings and their feathers froze to the rock, the way they were not able to move from it. And they

made such a hard struggle to get away, that they left the skin of their feet and their feathers and the tops of their wings on the rock after them.

'My grief, children of Lir,' said Fionnuala, 'it is bad our state is now, for we cannot bear the salt water to touch us, and there are bonds on us not to leave it; and if the salt water goes into our sores,' she said, 'we will get our death.' And she made this complaint:

'It is keening we are to-night; without feathers to cover our bodies; it is cold the rough, uneven rocks are under our bare feet.

'It is bad our stepmother was to us the time she played enchantments on us, sending us out like swans upon the sea.

'Our washing place is on the ridge of the bay, in the foam of flying manes of the sea; our share of the ale feast is the salt water of the blue tide.

'One daughter and three sons; it is in the clefts of the rocks we are; it is on the hard rocks we are, it is a pity the way we are.'

However, they came on to the course of the Maoil again, and the salt water was sharp and rough and bitter to them, but if it was itself, they were not able to avoid it or to get shelter from it. And they were there by the shore under that hardship till such time as their feathers grew again, and their wings, and till their sores were entirely healed. And then they used to go every day to the shore of Ireland or of Alban, but they had to come back to Sruth na Maoile every night.

Now they came one day to the mouth of the Banna, to the north of Ireland, and they saw a troop of riders, beautiful, of the one colour, with well-trained pure white horses under them, and they travelling the road straight from the south-west.

'Do you know who those riders are, sons of Lir?' said Fionnuala.

'We do not,' they said; 'but it is likely they might be some troop of the Sons of the Gael, or of the Tuatha de Danaan.'

They moved over closer to the shore then, that they might know who they were, and when the riders saw them they came to meet them until they were able to hold talk together.

And the chief men among them were two sons of Bodb Dearg, Aodh Aithfhiosach, of the quick wits, and Fergus Fithchiollach, of the chess, and a third part of the Riders of the Sidhe along with them, and it was for the swans they had been looking for a long while before that, and when they came together they wished one another a kind and loving welcome.

And the children of Lir asked for news of all the Men of Dea, and above all of Lir, and Bodb Dearg and their people.

'They are well, and they are in the one place together,' said they, 'in your father's house at Sidhe Fionnachaidh, using the Feast of Age pleasantly and happily, and with no uneasiness on them, only for being without yourselves, and without knowledge of what happened you from the day you left Loch Dairbhreach.'

'That has not been the way with us,' said Fionnuala, 'for we have gone through great hardship and uneasiness and misery on the tides of the sea until this day.'

And she made this complaint:

'There is delight to-night with the household of Lir! Plenty of ale with them and of wine, although it is in a cold dwelling-place this night are the four children of the king.

'It is without a spot our bedclothes are, our bodies covered over with curved feathers; but it is often we were dressed in purple, and we drinking pleasant mead.

'It is what our food is and our drink, the white sand and the bitter water of the sea; it is often we drank mead of hazel-nuts from round four-lipped drinking cups.

'It is what our beds are, bare rocks out of the power of the waves; it is often there used to be spread out for us beds of the breast-feathers of birds.

'Though it is our work now to be swimming through the frost and through the noise of the waves, it is often a company of the sons of kings were riding after us to the Hill of Bodb.

'It is what wasted my strength, to be going and coming over the current of the Maoil the way I never was used to, and never to be in the sunshine on the soft grass.

'Fiachra's bed and Conn's bed is to come under the cover of my wings on the sea. Aodh has his place under the feathers of my breast, the four of us side by side.

'The teaching of Manannán without deceit, the talk of Bodb Dearg on the pleasant ridge; the voice of Angus, his sweet kisses; it is by their side I used to be without grief.'

After that the riders went on to Lir's house, and they told the chief men of the Tuatha de Danaan all the birds had gone through, and the state they were in. 'We have no power over them,' the chief men said, 'but we are glad they are living yet, for they will get help in the end of time.'

As to the children of Lir, they went back towards their old place in the Maoil, and they stopped there till the time they had to spend in it was spent. And then Fionnuala said: 'The time is come for us to leave this place. And it is to Irrus Domnann we must go now,' she said, 'after our three hundred years here. And indeed there will be no rest for us there, or any standing ground, or any shelter from the storms. But since it is time for us to go, let us set out on the cold wind, the way we will not go astray.'

So they set out in that way, and left Sruth na Maoile behind them, and went to the point of Irrus Domnann, and there they stopped, and it is a life of misery and a cold life they led there. And one time the sea froze about them that they could not move at all, and the brothers were lamenting, and Fionnuala was comforting them, for she knew there would help come to them in the end.

And they stayed at Irrus Domnann till the time they had to spend there was spent. And then Fionnuala said: 'The time is come for us to go back to Sidhe Fionnachaidh, where our father is with his household and with all our own people.'

'It pleases us well to hear that,' they said.

So they set out flying through the air lightly till they came to Sidhe Fionnachaidh; and it is how they found the place, empty before them, and nothing in it but green hillocks and thickets of nettles, without a house, without a fire, without a hearthstone. And the four pressed close to one another then, and they gave out three sorrowful cries, and Fionnuala made this complaint:

'It is a wonder to me this place is, and it without a house, without a dwelling-place. To see it the way it is now, Ochone! it is bitterness to my heart.

'Without dogs, without hounds for hunting, without women, without great kings; we never knew it to be like this when our father was in it.

'Without horns, without cups, without drinking in the lighted house; without young men, without riders; the way it is to-night is a foretelling of sorrow.

'The people of the place to be as they are now, Ochone! it is grief to my heart! It is plain to my mind to-night the lord of the house is not living.

'Och, house where we used to see music and playing and the gathering of people! I think it a great change to see it lonely the way it is to-night.

'The greatness of the hardships we have gone through going from one wave to another of the sea, we never heard of the like of them coming on any other person.

'It is seldom this place had its part with grass and bushes; the man is not living that would know us, it would be a wonder to him to see us here.'

However, the children of Lir stopped that night in their father's place and their grandfather's, where they had been reared, and they were singing very sweet music of the Sidhe. And they rose up early on the morning of the morrow and went to Inis Gluaire, and all the birds of the country gathered near them on Loch na-n Ean, the Lake of the Birds. And they used to go out to feed every day to the far parts of the country, to Inis Geadh and to Accuill, the place Donn, son of Miled, and his people that were drowned were buried, and to all the western islands of Connacht, and they used to go back to Inis Gluaire every night.

It was about that time it happened them to meet with a young man of good race, and his name was Aibric; and he often took notice of the birds, and their singing was sweet to him and he loved them greatly, and they loved him. And it is this young man that told the whole story of all that had happened them, and put it in order.

And the story he told of what happened them in the end is this.

It was after the faith of Christ and blessed Patrick came into Ireland, that Saint Mochaomhog came to Inis Gluaire. And the first night he came to the island, the children of Lir heard the voice of his bell, ringing near them. And the brothers started up with fright when they heard it. 'We do not know,' they said, 'what is that weak, unpleasing voice we hear.'

'That is the voice of the bell of Mochaomhog,' said Fionnuala; 'and it is through that bell,' she said, 'you will be set free from pain and from misery.'

They listened to that music of the bell till the matins were done, and then they began to sing the low, sweet music of the Sidhe.

And Mochaomhog was listening to them, and he prayed to God to show him who was singing that music, and it was showed to him that the children of Lir were singing it. And on the morning of the morrow he went forward to the Lake of the Birds, and he saw the swans before him on the lake, and he went down to them at the brink of the shore. 'Are you the children of Lir?' he said.

'We are indeed,' said they.

'I give thanks to God for that,' said he, 'for it is for your sakes I am come to this island beyond any other island, and let you come to land now,' he said, 'and give your trust to me, that you may do good deeds and part from your sins.'

They came to the land after that, and they put trust in Mochaomhog, and he brought them to his own dwelling-place, and they used to be hearing Mass with him. And he got a good smith and bade him make chains of bright silver for them, and he put a chain between Aodh and Fionnuala, and a chain between Conn and Fiachra. And the four of them were raising his heart and gladdening

his mind, and no danger and no distress that was on the swans before put any trouble on them now.

Now the king of Connacht at that time was Lairgnen, son of Colman, son of Cobthach, and Deoch, daughter of Finghin, was his wife. And that was the coming together of the Man from the North and the Woman from the South, that Aoife had spoken of.

And the woman heard talk of the birds, and a great desire came on her to get them, and she bade Lairgnen to bring them to her, and he said he would ask them of Mochaomhog.

And she gave her word she would not stop another night with him unless he would bring them to her. And she set out from the house there and then. And Lairgnen sent messengers after her to bring her back, and they did not overtake her till she was at Cill Dun. She went back home with them then, and Lairgnen sent messengers to ask the birds of Mochaomhog, and he did not get them.

There was great anger on Lairgnen then, and he went himself to the place Mochaomhog was, and he asked was it true he had refused him the birds. 'It is true indeed,' said he. At that Lairgnen rose up, and he took hold of the swans, and pulled them off the altar, two birds in each hand, to bring them away to Deoch. But no sooner had he laid his hand on them than their bird skins fell off, and what was in their place was three lean, withered old men and a thin withered old woman, without blood or flesh.

And Lairgnen gave a great start at that, and he went out from the place. It is then Fionnuala said to Mochaomhog: 'Come and baptize us now, for it is short till our death comes; and it is certain you do not think worse of parting with us than we do of parting with you. And make our grave afterwards,' she said, 'and lay Conn at my right side and Fiachra on my left side, and Aodh before my face, between my two arms. And pray to the God of Heaven,' she said, 'that you may be able to baptize us.'

The children of Lir were baptized then, and they died and were buried as Fionnuala had desired; Fiachra and Conn one at each side of her, and Aodh before her face. And a stone was put over them, and their names were written in Ogham, and they were keened there, and heaven was gained for their souls.

And that is the fate of the children of Lir so far.

OISIN'S CHILDREN

By Lady Gregory

Now as to Oisin, that was so brave and so comely, and that could overtake a deer at its greatest speed, and see a thistle thorn on the darkest night, the wife he took was Eibhir of the plaited yellow hair, that was the foreign sweetheart of the High King of Ireland.

It is beyond the sea she lived, in a very sunny place; and her father's name was Iunsa, and her sunny house was thatched with the feathers of birds, and the doorposts were of gold, and the doors of ribbed grass. And Oisin went there looking for her, and he fought for her against the High King and against an army of the Firbolgs he had helping him; and he got the better of them all, and brought away Eibhir of the yellow hair to Ireland.

And he had a daughter that married the son of Oiliol, son of Eoghan, and of Beara, daughter of the King of Spain. It was that Eoghan was driven out of Ireland one time, and it is to Spain he went for safety. And Beara, that was daughter of the King of Spain, was very shining and beautiful, and her father had a mind to know who would be her husband, and he sent for his Druid and asked the question of him. 'I can tell you that,' said the Druid, 'for the man that is to be her husband will come to land in Spain this very night. And let your daughter go eastward to the river Eibhear,' he said, 'and she will find a crimson-spotted salmon in that river, having shining clothing on him from head to tail. And let her strip that clothing off him,' he said, 'and make with it a shining shirt for her husband.'

So Beara went to the river Eibhear, and found the golden salmon as the Druid had said, and she stripped him of his crimson clothing and made a shining shirt of it.

And as to Eoghan, the waves of the shore put a welcome before him, and he came the same night to the king's house. And the king gave him a friendly welcome; and it is what all the people said, that there was never seen a comelier man than Eoghan, or a woman more beautiful than Beara, and that it was fitting for them to come together. And Eoghan's own people said they would not be sorry for being sent away out of Ireland, if only Eoghan could get her for his wife.

And after a while the king sent his Druid to ask Eoghan why he did not ask for Beara. 'I will tell you that,' said Eoghan; 'it would not be fitting for me to be refused a wife, and I am but an exile in this country, and I have brought no treasures or goods with me out of Ireland for giving to learned men and to poets. But for all that,' he said, 'the king's daughter is dear to me, and I think I have the friendship of the king.'

The Druid went back with that message. 'That is the answer of a king,' said the King of Spain; 'and bid my daughter to sit at Eoghan's right hand,' he said, 'and I will give her to him this very night.' And when Beara, the king's daughter, heard that, she sent out her serving-

maid to bring the shirt she had made for Eoghan, and he put it on him over his armour, and its shining was seen in every place; and it was from wearing that shirt he got the name of Eoghan the Bright.

And Oiliol was the first son they had; it was he that had his ear bitten off by Aine of the Sidhe in revenge for her brother, and it was his son married Oisin's daughter afterwards.

And as to Osgar, that was Oisin's son, of all the young men of the Fianna he was the best in battle. And when he was but a young child he was made much of by the whole of the Fianna, and it is for him they used to keep the marrow bones, and they did not like to put any hardship on him. And he grew up tall and idle, and no one thought he would turn out so strong as he did. And one day there was an attack made on a troop of the Fianna, and all that were in it went out to fight, but they left Osgar after them. And when he knew the fight was going on, he took a log of wood that was the first thing he could find, and attacked the enemy and made a great slaughter, and they gave way and ran before him. And from that out there was no battle he did not go into; and he was said to be the strongest of all the Fianna, though the people of Connacht said that Goll was the strongest. And he and Diarmuid, grandson of Duibhne, were comrades and dear friends; and it was Diarmuid taught him feats of arms and of skill, and chess-playing. And Oisin his father took great pride in him, and his grandfather Finn. And one time Finn was holding a feast at Almhuin, and he asked the chief men of the Fianna that were there what was the music they thought the best. 'To be playing at games,' said Conan, 'that is the best music I ever heard;' for though Conan was a good hand against an enemy, there never was a man had less sense. 'The music I like the best is to be talking with a woman,' said Diarmuid. 'My music is the outcry of my hounds, and they putting a deer to its last stand,' said Lugaidh's son. 'The music of the woods is best to me,' said Oisin; 'the sound of the wind and of the cuckoo and the blackbird, and the sweet silence of the crane.'

And then Osgar was asked, and he said: 'The best music is the striking of swords in a battle.' And it is likely he took after Finn in that, for in spite of all the sweet sounds he gave an account of the time he was at Conan's house, at Ceann Slieve, it used to be said by the Fianna that the music that was best with Finn was what happened.

This now is the way Osgar met with his wife.

One time Finn and his men came to Slieve Crot, and they saw a woman waiting there before them, having a crimson fringed cloak, and a gold brooch in it, and a band of yellow gold on her forehead. Finn asked her name, and where she came from. 'Etain of the Fair Hair is my name,' she said, 'daughter of Aedh of the White Breast, of the hill of the Sidhe at Beinn Edair, son of Angus Og.' 'What is it brought you here, girl?' said Finn. 'To ask a man of the Fianna of Ireland to run a race with me.' 'What sort of a runner are you?' said Diarmuid. 'I am a good runner,' said the girl; 'for it is the same to me if the ground is long or short under my feet.'

All of the Fianna that were there then set out to run with her, and they ran to the height over Badhamair and on to Ath Cliath, and from that on to the hill of the Sidhe at Beinn Edair.

And there was a good welcome before them, and they were brought meat and wine for drinking, and water for washing their feet. And after a while they saw a nice fair-haired girl in front of the

vats, and a cup of white silver in her hand, and she giving out drink to every one. 'It seems to me that is the girl came asking the Fianna to race against her at Slieve Crot,' said Finn. 'It is not,' said Aedh of the White Breast, 'for that is the slowest woman there is among us.' 'Who was it so?' said Finn. 'It was Be-mannair, daughter of Ainceol, woman-messenger of the Tuatha de Danaan. And it is she that changes herself into all shapes; and she will take the shape of a fly, and of a true lover, and every one leaves their secret with her. And it was she outran you coming from the east,' he said, 'and not this other girl that was drinking and making merry here in the hall.' 'What is her name?' said Finn. 'Etain of the Fair Hair,' he said; 'a daughter of my own, and a darling of the Tuatha de Danaan. And it is the way with her, she has a lover of the men of the Fianna.' 'That is well,' said Finn; 'and who is that lover?' 'It is Osgar, son of Oisin,' said Aedh; 'and it is she herself sent her messenger for you,' he said, 'in her own shape, to Slieve Crot in the south. And the son of the High King of Ireland has offered a great bride-price to the Men of Dea for her,' he said, 'three hundreds of the land nearest to Bregia and to Midhe, and to put himself and his weight of gold into a balance, and to give it all to her. But we did not take it,' he said, 'since she had no mind or wish for it herself, and so we made no dealing or agreement about her.' 'Well,' said Finn, 'and what conditions will you ask of Osgar?' 'Never to leave me for anything at all but my own fault,' said the girl. 'I will make that agreement with you indeed,' said Osgar. 'Give me sureties for it,' said she; 'give me the sureties of Goll for the sons of Morna, and of Finn, son of Cumhal, for the Fianna of Ireland.'

So they gave those sureties, and the wedding-feast was made, and they stopped there for twenty nights. And at the end of that time

Osgar asked Finn where would he bring his wife. 'Bring her to wide Almhuin for the first seven years,' said Finn.

But a while after that, in a great battle at Beinn Edair, Osgar got so heavy a wound that Finn and the Fianna were as if they had lost their wits. And when Etain of the Fair Hair came to the bed where Osgar was lying, and saw the way he was, and that the great kinglike shape he had was gone from him, greyness and darkness came on her, and she raised pitiful cries, and she went to her bed and her heart broke in her like a nut; and she died of grief for her husband and her first love.

But it was not at that time Osgar got his death, but afterwards in the battle of Gabhra.

BALOR ON TORY ISLAND

By Jeremiah Curtin

Long ago Ri Balor lived on Tory Island, and he lived there because it was prophesied that he was never to die unless he'd be killed by the son of his only daughter.

Balor, to put the daughter in the way that she'd never have a son, went to live on Tory, and built a castle on Tor Mor, a cliff jutting into the ocean. He put twelve women to guard the daughter, and all around the castle he had cords fixed, and every one of them tied to bells, so that no man could come in secret. If any man touched a cord all the bells would ring and give notice, and Balor would seize him.

Balor lived that way, well satisfied. He was full sure that his life was out of danger.

Opposite on the mainland, at Druim na Teine (hill of fire), lived a smith, Gavidin, who had his forge there. The smith owned a cow called Glas Gavlen, and she was his enchanted step-sister.

This cow was called Gavlen because she was giving milk, and she the fifth year without a calf. Glas Gavlen was very choice of food; she would eat no grass but the best. But if the cow ate much good grass there was no measuring the milk she gave; she filled every vessel, and the milk was sweet and rich.

The smith set great value on Glas Gavlen, and no wonder, for she was the first cow that came to Erin, and at that time the only one.

The smith took care of the cow himself, and never let her out of his sight except when working in his forge, and then he had a careful man minding her.

Balor had an eye on Glas Gavlen, and wanted to bring her to Tory for his own use, so he told two agents of his, Maol and Mullag, who were living near Druim na Teine, to get the cow for him. The smith would not part with Glas Gavlen for any price, so there was no way left but to steal her. There was no chance for stealing till one time when three brothers, named Duv, Donn, and Fin, sons of Ceanfaeligh (Kinealy), went to the forge to have three swords made.

'Each man of you is to mind the cow while I am working,' said the smith, 'and if he loses her I'll take the head off him.'

'We will agree to that,' said the brothers.

Duv and Donn went with Glas Gavlen on the first day and the second, and brought her back to the smith safely. When his turn came Fin took the cow out on the third day, but when some distance from the forge he bethought himself and ran back to tell the smith not to make his sword so heavy as those of his brothers. The moment he was inside in the forge Maol and Mullag, Balor's men, stole the cow, and away they went quickly, driving her toward Baile Nass. When they came to the brow of the slope, where the sand begins, they drew her down to the water's edge by the tail, and put her into a boat which they had there prepared and ready.

They sailed toward Tory, but stopped at Inis Bofin (island of the

white cow) and put the cow out on land. She drank from a well there, which is called since that time Tobar na Glaise (well of the grey cow). After that they sailed on, and landed the same day at Port na Glaise, on Tory Island.

When Fin came out of the forge he saw nothing of Glas Gavlen, – neither trace nor sign of her. He ran back then with the evil tidings to the smith.

'If you fail to bring her back to me within three days,' said Gavidin, 'I'll take the head off you, according to our bargain. I made the sword to oblige you, and you promised to bring the cow or give your head.'

Away with Fin then, travelling and lamenting, looking for Glas Gavlen. He went toward Baile Nass and came to a place on the strand where a party of men were playing ball. He inquired of them about the cow, but they began to make game of him, he looked so queer in himself, and was so sad. At last one of the players, whose name was Gial Duv (Black Jaw), came up to Fin and spoke to him: 'Stand aside till the game is over, and I'll talk to you. This is a party of players that you should not interfere with; they are lucht sidhe (people of the mounds, fairies). I know what your trouble is. I will go with you, and do my best to bring the cow. I know where she is, and if I cannot bring her, no one can.'

They searched down as far as Maheroerty, and went then to Minlara, where a boat was found. They sailed away in the boat, and reached Tory that night a few hours after Maol and Mullag.

'Go now,' said Gial Duv to Fin, 'and ask Balor what would release the cow, and what can you do to earn her. I'll stay here till you come back to me.'

Fin went to Balor and asked the question.

'To get the cow,' said Balor, 'you must eat seven green hides while one inch of a rush-light is burning, and I'll light it myself.'

Fin returned and told Gial Duv. 'Go,' said Gial, 'and tell him you will try to do that. He will put you in a room apart with the hides and take the rush himself. Cut the hides quickly, and if you can cut them I'll make away with them. I'll be there with you, invisible.'

All this was done. Fin cut the hides and Gial Duv put them away. The moment the rush-light was burned Balor came in, and there wasn't a hand's breadth of the hides left.

'I have the seven hides eaten,' said Fin.

'Come to me to-morrow. My daughter will throw the cow's halter. If she throws it to you the cow will be yours.'

Fin was let out of the room then.

'Now,' said Gial Duv, 'I'll take you to Balor's daughter. There is a wall between the castle and the rest of the island, and I'll take you over it. There are cords along the wall everywhere, and whoever tries to pass over will touch them and sound all the bells in the place. I will raise you above them all and take you in without noise. You will go first to Balor's daughter; she will be pleased with you and like you. After that you will see all the other women, and do you be as intimate with them as with Balor's daughter, so that they will not tell that you were in it, and be sure to tell the daughter to throw you the cow's halter tomorrow.'

Fin was taken into the castle by Gial Duv without noise, and he did all that Gial directed. Next day Fin went to Balor and asked for the cow.

'Well, come with me. Let my daughter throw the halter. If she throws it to you the cow will be yours.'

They went. She threw the halter at Fin, and Balor was very angry. 'Oh, daughter,' cried he, 'what have you done?'

'Don't you know,' said she, 'that there is a false cast in every woman's hand? There is a crooked vein in my arm, and I could not help it; that's what gave the halter to Fin.'

Balor had to give the cow and forgive the daughter. Fin took Glas Gavlen to the mainland that day and gave her to the smith.

Before the year was out Gial Duv went to Fin and said, 'Make ready and come with me to Tory; if you don't Balor will find out what happened when you were on the island, and kill his own daughter, with the twelve women and all the children.'

The two went to Tory that evening, and when the children were born the women gave twelve of them to Fin in a blanket, and one, Balor's grandson, by himself in a separate cloth. Fin took his place in the boat with the twelve on his back, and one at his breast. The blanket was fastened at his throat with a dealg (thorn); the thorn broke (there was a great stress on it, for the weather was rough), and the twelve children fell in the water at Sruth Deilg and became seals.

'Oh!' cried Gial, 'the children are lost. Have you Balor's grandson?'

'I have,' answered Fin.

'That is well. We don't care for the others while we have him.'

They brought the child to the mainland, where a nurse was found, but the child was not thriving with her.

'Let us return to Tory with the boy,' said Gial Duv. 'There is nothing that Balor wishes for so much as trees. He has tried often to make trees grow on the island, but it was no use for him. Do you promise that you'll make a grand forest on Tory if he'll let some of the women nurse the child. Tell him that your wife died not long ago. Balor will say, "How could we find a nurse here when there is no woman on the island who has a child of her own?" You will say that 'tis a power this child has that whatever woman touches him has her breast full of milk. I will put you in with the women in the evening, and do you tell them what is wanted. The mother is to take the child first when you go in to-morrow, and she will hand him quickly to another and that one to a third, and so on before any can be stopped.'

Fin gave the child to Balor's daughter before her father could come near her; she gave him to one of the women, and he was passed on till all twelve had had him. It was found that all had milk, and Balor consented to let the child be nursed.

Gial Duv made a large fine forest of various trees. For two years Balor was delighted; he was the gladdest man, for all he wanted was trees and shelter on Tory Island.

The child was in good hands now with his mother and the twelve women, and when able to walk, Fin used to bring him out in the daytime. Once he kept him and went to the mainland. The next day a terrible wind rose, and it didn't leave a tree standing on Tory. Balor knew now that the forest was all enchantment and deceit, and said that he would destroy Fin and all his clan for playing such a trick on him. Balor sent his agents and servants to watch Fin and kill him.

Fin was warned by Gial Duv, and took care of himself for a long time, but at last they caught him. It was his custom to hunt in Glen Ath, for there were many deer and much game there in those days, and Fin was very fond of hunting; but he shunned all their ambushes, till one evening when they were lying in wait for him in the bushes

by a path which he was travelling for the first time. They leaped up when he was near, caught him, and bound him.

'Take the head off me at one blow,' said he, 'and be done with it.'

They put his head on a stone and cut it off with one blow. In this way died Fin MacKinealy, the father of Balor's grandson. This grandson was a strong youth now. He was a young man, in fact, and his name was Lui Lavada (Lui Longhand). He was called Lavada because his arms were so long that he could tie his shoes without stooping. Lui did not know that he was Balor's grandson. He knew that his father had been killed by Balor's men, and he was waiting to avenge him.

A couple of years later there was a wedding on the mainland, and it was the custom that no one was to begin to eat at a wedding till Maol and Mullag should carve the first slices. They did not come this time in season, and all the guests were impatient.

'I'll carve the meat for you,' said Balor's grandson. With that he carved some slices, and all present began to eat and drink.

After a while Maol and Mullag came, and they were in a great rage because the people were eating, drinking, and enjoying the wedding feast without themselves.

When all had finished eating and drinking, and were ready to go home, Maol said, 'The bride will go with me.'

The bride began to cry when she heard that, and was in great distress. Lui Lavada asked what trouble was on her, and the people told him, that since Balor's two deputies were ruling on the mainland it was their custom at weddings that Maol, the first in authority, should keep company with the bride the first evening, and Mullag the second evening.

'It's time to put a stop to that,' said Lui Lavada, Balor's grandson. With that he walked up to the two and said, 'Ye'll go home out of this as ye are.'

Maol answered with insult, and made an offer to strike him. Lui caught Maol then and split his tongue; he cut a hole in each of his cheeks, and putting one half of the tongue through the left cheek, and the other through the right, he thrust a sliver of wood through the tips of each half. He took Mullag then and treated him in like manner.

The people led the two down to the seashore after that. Lui put Maol in one boat and Mullag in another, and let them go with the wind, which carried them out in the ocean, and there is no account that any man saved them.

Balor swore vengeance on the people for destroying his men, and especially on Lui Lavada. He had an eye in the middle of his forehead which he kept covered always with nine shields of thick leather, so that he might not open his eye and turn it on anything, for no matter what Balor looked at with the naked eye he burned it to ashes. He set out in a rage then from Tory, and never stopped till he landed at Baile Nass and went toward Gavidin's forge. The grandson was there before him, and had a spear ready and red hot.

When Balor had eight shields raised from the evil eye, and was just raising the ninth, Lui Lavada sent the red spear into it. Balor pursued his grandson, who retreated before him, going south, and never stopped till he reached Dun Lui, near Errigal Mountain. There he sat on a rock, wearied and exhausted. While he was sitting there, everything came to his mind that he did since the time that his men stole Glas Gavlen from Gavidin Gow. 'I see it all now,' said he. 'This is

my grandson who has given the mortal blow to me. He is the son of my daughter and Fin MacKinealy. No one else could have given that spear cast but him.' With that Balor called to the grandson and said, 'Come near now. Take the head off me and place it above on your own a few moments. You will know everything in the world, and no one will be able to conquer you.'

Lui took the head off his grandfather, and, instead of putting it on his own head, he put it on a rock. The next moment a drop came out of the head, made a thousand pieces of the rock, and dug a hole in the earth three times deeper than Loch Foyle – the deepest lake in the world up to that time – and so long that in that hole are the waters of Gweedore Loch, they have been there from that day to this.

* * * * *

The above tale I wrote down on the mainland, where I found also another version, but inferior to this. On Tory itself I found two versions, both incomplete. Though differing in particulars, the argument is the same in all. Balor is represented as living on Tory to escape the doom which threatens him through a coming grandson; he covets the cow Glas Gavlen, and finally gains her through his agents.

The theft of the cow is the first act in a series which ends with the death of Balor at Gweedore, and brings about the fulfilment of the prophecy. In all the variants of the tale Balor is the same unrepentant, unconquerable character – the man whom nothing can bend, who tries to avenge his own fate after his death by the destruction of his grandson. The grandson does not know whom he is about to kill. He slays Balor to avenge his father, Fin MacKinealy, according to the vendetta of the time.

THE BIRTH OF FIN MACCUMHAIL[1]

By Jeremiah Curtin

Cumhal Macart was a great champion in the west of Erin, and it was prophesied of him that if ever he married he would meet death in the next battle he fought.

For this reason he had no wife, and knew no woman for a long time; till one day he saw the king's daughter, who was so beautiful that he forgot all fear and married her in secret.

Next day after the marriage, news came that a battle had to be fought.

Now a Druid had told the king that his daughter's son would take the kingdom from him; so he made up his mind to look after the daughter, and not let any man come near her.

Before he went to the battle, Cumhal told his mother everything – told her of his relations with the king's daughter.

He said, 'I shall be killed in battle to-day, according to the prophecy

---

[1] Cumhail, genitive of Cumhal, after Mac = son; pronounced Cool.

of the Druid, and I'm afraid if his daughter has a son the king will kill the child, for the prophecy is that he will lose the kingdom by the son of his own daughter. Now, if the king's daughter has a son do you hide and rear him, if you can; you will be his only hope and stay.'

Cumhal was killed in the battle, and within that year the king's daughter had a son. By command of his grandfather, the boy was thrown out of the castle window into a loch, to be drowned, on the day of his birth.

The boy sank from sight; but after remaining a while under the water, he rose again to the surface, and came to land holding a live salmon in his hand.

The grandmother of the boy, Cumhal's mother, stood watching on the shore, and said to herself as she saw this: 'He is my grandson, the true son of my own child,' and seizing the boy, she rushed away with him, and vanished, before the king's people could stop her.

When the king heard that the old woman had escaped with his daughter's son, he fell into a terrible rage, and ordered all the male children born that day in the kingdom to be put to death, hoping in this way to kill his own grandson, and save the crown for himself.

After she had disappeared from the bank of the loch, the old woman, Cumhal's mother, made her way to a thick forest, where she spent that night as best she could. Next day she came to a great oak tree. Then she hired a man to cut out a chamber in the tree.

When all was finished, and there was a nice room in the oak for herself and her grandson, and a whelp of the same age as the boy, and which she had brought with her from the castle, she said to the man: 'Give me the axe which you have in your hand, there is something here that I want to fix.'

The man gave the axe into her hand, and that minute she swept the head off him, saying: 'You'll never tell any man about this place now.'

One day the whelp ate some of the fine chippings (*bran*) left cut by the carpenter from the inside of the tree. The old woman said: 'You'll be called Bran from this out.'

All three lived in the tree together, and the old woman did not take her grandson out till the end of five years; and then he couldn't walk, he had been sitting so long inside.

When the old grandmother had taught the boy to walk, she brought him one day to the brow of a hill from which there was a long slope. She took a switch and said: 'Now, run down this place. I will follow and strike you with this switch, and coming up I will run ahead, and you strike me as often as you can.'

The first time they ran down, his grandmother struck him many times. In coming up the first time, he did not strike her at all. Every time they ran down she struck him less, and every time they ran up he struck her more.

They ran up and down for three days; and at the end of that time she could not strike him once, and he struck her at every step she took. He had now become a great runner.

When he was fifteen years of age, the old woman went with him to a hurling match between the forces of his grandfather and those of a neighbouring king. Both sides were equal in skill; and neither was able to win, till the youth opposed his grandfather's people. Then, he won every game. When the ball was thrown in the air, he struck it coming down, and so again and again – never letting the ball touch the ground till he had driven it through the barrier.

The old king, who was very angry, and greatly mortified, at the defeat of his people, exclaimed, as he saw the youth, who was very fair and had white hair: 'Who is that *fin cumhal*[2] (white cap)?'

'Ah, that is it; Fin will be his name, and Fin MacCumhail he is,' said the old woman.

The king ordered his people to seize and put the young man to death, on the spot. The old woman hurried to the side of her grandson. They slipped from the crowd and away they went, a hill at a leap, a glen at a step, and thirty-two miles at a running-leap. They ran a long distance, till Fin grew tired; then the old grandmother took him on her back, putting his feet into two pockets which were in her dress, one on each side, and ran on with the same swiftness as before, a hill at a leap, a glen at a step, and thirty-two miles at a running-leap.

After a time, the old woman felt the approach of pursuit, and said to Fin: 'Look behind, and tell me what you see.'

'I see,' said he, 'a white horse with a champion on his back.'

'Oh, no fear,' said she; 'a white horse has no endurance; he can never catch us, we are safe from him.' And on they sped. A second time she felt the approach of pursuit, and again she said: 'Look back, and see who is coming.'

Fin looked back, and said: 'I see a warrior riding on a brown horse.'

'Never fear,' said the old woman; 'there is never a brown horse but is giddy, he cannot overtake us.' She rushed on as before. A third time she said: 'Look around, and see who is coming now.'

2 Cumhal, the name of Fin's father. Denotes also a cap or head-covering, fin = white. The punning resemblance suggested to the old woman the full name, Fin MacCumhail.

Fin looked, and said: 'I see a black warrior on a black horse, following fast.'

'There is no horse so tough as a black horse,' said the grandmother. 'There is no escape from this one. My grandson, one or both of us must die. I am old, my time has nearly come. I will die, and you and Bran save yourselves. (Bran had been with them all the time.) Right here ahead is a deep bog; you jump off my back, and escape as best you can. I'll jump into the bog up to my neck; and when the king's men come, I'll say that you are in the bog before me, sunk out of sight, and I'm trying to find you. As my hair and yours are the same colour, they will think my head good enough to carry back. They will cut it off, and take it in place of yours, and show it to the king; that will satisfy his anger.'

Fin slipped down, took farewell of his grandmother, and hurried on with Bran. The old woman came to the bog, jumped in, and sank to her neck. The king's men were soon at the edge of the bog, and the black rider called out to the old woman: 'Where is Fin?'

'He is here in the bog before me, and I'm trying can I find him.'

As the horsemen could not find Fin, and thought the old woman's head would do to carry back, they cut it off, and took it with them, saying: 'This will satisfy the king.'

Fin and Bran went on till they came to a great cave, in which they found a herd of goats. At the further end of the cave was a smouldering fire. The two lay down to rest.

A couple of hours later, in came a giant with a salmon in his hand. This giant was of awful height, he had but one eye, and that in the middle of his forehead, as large as the sun in heaven.

When he saw Fin, he called out: 'Here, take this salmon and roast it; but be careful, for if you raise a single blister on it I'll cut the head off you. I've followed this salmon for three days and three nights without stopping, and I never let it out of my sight, for it is the most wonderful salmon in the world.'

The giant lay down to sleep in the middle of the cave. Fin spitted the salmon, and held it over the fire.

The minute the giant closed the one eye in his head, he began to snore. Every time he drew breath into his body, he dragged Fin, the spit, the salmon, Bran, and all the goats to his mouth; and every time he drove a breath out of himself, he threw them back to the places they were in before. Fin was drawn time after time to the mouth of the giant with such force, that he was in dread of going down his throat.

When partly cooked, a blister rose on the salmon. Fin pressed the place with his thumb, to know could he break the blister, and hide from the giant the harm that was done. But he burned his thumb, and, to ease the pain, put it between his teeth, and gnawed the skin to the flesh, the flesh to the bone, the bone to the marrow; and when he had tasted the marrow, he received the knowledge of all things. Next moment, he was drawn by the breath of the giant right up to his face, and, knowing from his thumb what to do, he plunged the hot spit into the sleeping eye of the giant and destroyed it.

That instant the giant with a single bound was at the low entrance of the cave, and, standing with his back to the wall and a foot on each side of the opening, roared out: 'You'll not leave this place alive.'

Now Fin killed the largest goat, skinned him as quickly as he could, then putting the skin on himself he drove the herd to where the giant stood; the goats passed out one by one between his legs.

When the great goat came the giant took him by the horns. Fin slipped from the skin, and ran out.

'Oh, you've escaped,' said the giant, 'but before we part let me make you a present.'

'I'm afraid to go near you,' said Fin; 'if you wish to give me a present, put it out this way, and then go back.'

The giant placed a ring on the ground, then went back. Fin took up the ring and put it on the end of his little finger above the first joint. It clung so firmly that no man in the world could have taken it off.

The giant then called out, 'Where are you?'

'On Fin's finger,' cried the ring. That instant the giant sprang at Fin and almost came down on his head, thinking in this way to crush him to bits. Fin sprang to a distance. Again the giant asked, 'Where are you?'

'On Fin's finger,' answered the ring.

Again the giant made a leap, coming down just in front of Fin. Many times he called and many times almost caught Fin, who could not escape with the ring on his finger. While in this terrible struggle, not knowing how to escape, Bran ran up and asked:

'Why don't you chew your thumb?'

Fin bit his thumb to the marrow, and then knew what to do. He took the knife with which he had skinned the goat, cut off his finger at the first joint, and threw it, with the ring still on, into a deep bog near by.

Again the giant called out, 'Where are you?' and the ring answered, 'On Fin's finger.'

Straightway the giant sprang towards the voice, sank to his shoulders in the bog, and stayed there.

Fin with Bran now went on his way, and travelled till he reached a deep and thick wood, where a thousand horses were drawing timber, and men felling and preparing it.

'What is this?' asked Fin of the overseer of the workmen.

'Oh, we are building a dun (a castle) for the king; we build one every day, and every night it is burned to the ground. Our king has an only daughter; he will give her to any man who will save the dun, and he'll leave him the kingdom at his death. If any man undertakes to save the dun and fails, his life must pay for it; the king will cut his head off. The best champions in Erin have tried and failed; they are now in the king's dungeons, a whole army of them, waiting the king's pleasure. He's going to cut the heads off them all in one day.'

'Why don't you chew your thumb?' asked Bran.

Fin chewed his thumb to the marrow, and then knew that on the eastern side of the world there lived an old hag with her three sons, and every evening at nightfall she sent the youngest of these to burn the king's dun.

'I will save the king's dun,' said Fin.

'Well,' said the overseer, 'better men than you have tried and lost their lives.'

'Oh,' said Fin, 'I'm not afraid; I'll try for the sake of the king's daughter.'

Now Fin, followed by Bran, went with the overseer to the king. 'I hear you will give your daughter to the man who saves your dun,' said Fin.

'I will,' said the king; 'but if he fails I must have his head.'

'Well,' said Fin, 'I'll risk my head for the sake of your daughter. If

I fail I'm satisfied.' The king gave Fin food and drink; he supped, and after supper went to the dun.

'Why don't you chew your thumb?' said Bran; 'then you'll know what to do.' He did. Then Bran took her place on the roof, waiting for the old woman's son. Now the old woman in the east told her youngest son to hurry on with his torches, burn the dun, and come back without delay; for the stirabout was boiling and he must not be too late for supper.

He took the torches, and shot off through the air with a wonderful speed. Soon he was in sight of the king's dun, threw the torches upon the thatched roof to set it on fire as usual.

That moment Bran gave the torches such a push with her shoulders, that they fell into the stream which ran around the dun, and were put out. 'Who is this,' cried the youngest son of the old hag, 'who has dared to put out my lights, and interfere with my hereditary right?'

'I,' said Fin, who stood in front of him. Then began a terrible battle between Fin and the old woman's son. Bran came down from the dun to help Fin; she bit and tore his enemy's back, stripping the skin and flesh from his head to his heels.

After a terrible struggle such as had not been in the world before that night, Fin cut the head off his enemy. But for Bran, Fin could never have conquered.

The time for the return of her son had passed; supper was ready. The old woman, impatient and angry, said to the second son: 'You take torches and hurry on, see why your brother loiters. I'll pay him for this when he comes home! But be careful and don't do like him, or you'll have your pay too. Hurry back, for the stirabout is boiling and ready for supper.'

He started off, was met and killed exactly as his brother, except that he was stronger and the battle fiercer. But for Bran, Fin would have lost his life that night.

The old woman was raging at the delay, and said to her eldest son, who had not been out of the house for years: (It was only in case of the greatest need that she sent him. He had a cat's head, and was called Pus an Chuine, 'Puss of the Corner;' he was the eldest and strongest of all the brothers.) 'Now take torches, go and see what delays your brothers; I'll pay them for this when they come home.'

The eldest brother shot off through the air, came to the king's dun, and threw his torches upon the roof. They had just singed the straw a little, when Bran pushed them off with such force that they fell into the stream and were quenched.

'Who is this,' screamed Cat-head, 'who dares to interfere with my ancestral right?'

'I,' shouted Fin. Then the struggle began fiercer than with the second brother. Bran helped from behind, tearing the flesh from his head to his heels; but at length Cat-head fastened his teeth into Fin's breast, biting and gnawing till Fin cut the head off. The body fell to the ground, but the head lived, gnawing as terribly as before. Do what they could it was impossible to kill it. Fin hacked and cut, but could neither kill nor pull it off. When nearly exhausted, Bran said:

'Why don't you chew your thumb?'

Fin chewed his thumb, and reaching the marrow knew that the old woman in the east was ready to start with torches to find her sons, and burn the dun herself, and that she had a vial of liquid with which she could bring the sons to life; and that nothing could free him from Cat-head but the old woman's blood.

After midnight the old hag, enraged at the delay of her sons, started and shot through the air like lightning, more swiftly than her sons. She threw her torches from afar upon the roof of the dun; but Bran as before hurled them into the stream.

Now the old woman circled around in the air looking for her sons. Fin was getting very weak from pain and loss of blood, for Cat-head was biting at his breast all the time.

Bran called out: 'Rouse yourself, oh, Fin; use all your power or we are lost! If the old hag gets a drop from the vial upon the bodies of her sons, they will come to life, and then we're done for.'

Thus roused, Fin with one spring reached the old woman in the air, and swept the bottle from her grasp; which falling upon the ground was emptied.

The old hag gave a scream which was heard all over the world, came to the ground and closed with Fin. Then followed a battle greater than the world had ever known before that night, or has ever seen since. Water sprang out of grey rocks, cows cast their calves even when they had none, and hard rushes grew soft in the remotest corner of Erin, so desperate was the fighting and so awful, between Fin and the old hag. Fin would have died that night but for Bran.

Just as daylight was coming Fin swept the head off the old woman, caught some of her blood, and rubbed it around Cat-head, who fell off dead.

He rubbed his own wounds with the blood and was cured; then rubbed some on Bran, who had been singed with the torches, and she was as well as ever. Fin, exhausted with fighting, dropped down and fell asleep.

While he was sleeping the chief steward of the king came to the dun, found it standing safe and sound, and seeing Fin lying there asleep knew that he had saved it. Bran tried to waken Fin, pulled and tugged, but could not rouse him.

The steward went to the king, and said: 'I have saved the dun, and I claim the reward.'

'It shall be given you,' answered the king; and straightway the steward was recognized as the king's son-in-law, and orders were given to make ready for the wedding.

Bran had listened to what was going on, and when her master woke, exactly at midday, she told him of all that was taking place in the castle of the king.

Fin went to the king, and said: 'I have saved your dun, and I claim the reward.'

'Oh,' said the king, 'my steward claimed the reward, and it has been given to him.'

'He had nothing to do with saving the dun; I saved it,' said Fin.

'Well,' answered the king, 'he is the first man who told me of its safety and claimed the reward.'

'Bring him here: let me look at him,' said Fin.

He was sent for, and came. 'Did you save the king's dun?' asked Fin. 'I did,' said the steward.

'You did not, and take that for your lies,' said Fin; and striking him with the edge of his open hand he swept the head off his body, dashing it against the other side of the room, flattening it like paste on the wall.

'You are the man,' said the king to Fin, 'who saved the dun; yours

is the reward. All the champions, and there is many a man of them, who have failed to save it are in the dungeons of my fortress; their heads must be cut off before the wedding takes place.'

'Will you let me see them?' asked Fin.

'I will,' said the king.

Fin went down to the men, and found the first champions of Erin in the dungeons. 'Will you obey me in all things if I save you from death?' said Fin. 'We will,' said they. Then he went back to the king and asked:

'Will you give me the lives of these champions of Erin, in place of your daughter's hand?'

'I will,' said the king.

All the champions were liberated, and left the king's castle that day. Ever after they followed the orders of Fin, and these were the beginning of his forces and the first of the Fenians of Erin.

FIN MACCUMHAIL AND THE FENIANS OF ERIN IN THE CASTLE OF FEAR DUBH

By Jeremiah Curtin

It was the custom with Fin MacCumhail and the Fenians of Erin, when a stranger from any part of the world came to their castle, not to ask him a question for a year and a day.

On a time, a champion came to Fin and his men, and remained with them. He was not at all pleasant or agreeable.

At last Fin and his men took counsel together; they were much annoyed because their guest was so dull and morose, never saying a word, always silent.

While discussing what kind of man he was, Diarmuid Duivne offered to try him; so one evening when they were eating together, Diarmuid came and snatched from his mouth the hind-quarter of a bullock, which he was picking.

Diarmuid pulled at one part of the quarter – pulled with all his strength, but only took the part that he seized, while the other kept

the part he held. All laughed; the stranger laughed too, as heartily as any. It was the first laugh they had heard from him.

The strange champion saw all their feats of arms and practised with them, till the year and a day were over. Then he said to Fin and his men:

'I have spent a pleasant year in your company; you gave me good treatment, and the least I can do now is to give you a feast at my own castle.'

No one had asked what his name was up to that time. Fin now asked his name. He answered: 'My name is Fear Dubh, of Alba.'

Fin accepted the invitation; and they appointed the day for the feast, which was to be in Erin, since Fear Dubh did not wish to trouble them to go to Alban. He took leave of his host and started for home.

When the day for the feast came, Fin and the chief men of the Fenians of Erin set out for the castle of Fear Dubh.

They went, a glen at a step, a hill at a leap, and thirty-two miles at a running leap, till they came to the grand castle where the feast was to be given.

They went in; everything was ready, seats at the table, and every man's name at his seat in the same order as at Fin's castle. Diarmuid, who was always very sportive – fond of hunting, and paying court to women, was not with them; he had gone to the mountains with his dogs.

All sat down, except Conan Maol MacMorna (never a man spoke well of him); no seat was ready for him, for he used to lie on the flat of his back on the floor, at Fin's castle.

When all were seated the door of the castle closed of itself. Fin then asked the man nearest the door, to rise and open it. The man tried to rise; he pulled this way and that, over and hither, but he couldn't get up. Then the next man tried, and the next, and so on, till the turn came to Fin himself, who tried in vain.

Now, whenever Fin and his men were in trouble and great danger it was their custom to raise a cry of distress (a voice of howling), heard all over Erin. Then all men knew that they were in peril of death; for they never raised this cry except in the last extremity.

Fin's son, Fialan, who was three years old and in the cradle, heard the cry, was roused, and jumped up.

'Get me a sword!' said he to the nurse. 'My father and his men are in distress; I must go to aid them.'

'What could you do, poor little child.'

Fialan looked around, saw an old rusty sword-blade laid aside for ages. He took it down, gave it a snap; it sprang up so as to hit his arm, and all the rust dropped off; the blade was pure as shining silver.

'This will do,' said he; and then he set out towards the place where he heard the cry, going a glen at a step, a hill at a leap, and thirty-two miles at a running leap, till he came to the door of the castle, and cried out.

Fin answered from inside, 'Is that you, my child?'

'It is,' said Fialan.

'Why did you come?'

'I heard your cry, and how could I stay at home, hearing the cry of my father and the Fenians of Erin!'

'Oh, my child, you cannot help us much.'

Fialan struck the door powerfully with his sword, but no use. Then, one of the men inside asked Fin to chew his thumb, to know what was keeping them in, and why they were bound.

Fin chewed his thumb, from skin to blood, from blood to bone, from bone to marrow, and discovered that Fear Dubh had built the castle by magic, and that he was coming himself with a great force to cut the head off each one of them. (These men from Alba had always a grudge against the champions of Erin.)

Said Fin to Fialan: 'Do you go now, and stand at the ford near the castle, and meet Fear Dubh.'

Fialan went and stood in the middle of the ford. He wasn't long there when he saw Fear Dubh coming with a great army.

'Leave the ford, my child,' said Fear Dubh, who knew him at once. 'I have not come to harm your father. I spent a pleasant year at his castle. I've only come to show him honour.'

'I know why you have come,' answered Fialan. 'You've come to destroy my father and all his men, and I'll not leave this ford while I can hold it.'

'Leave the ford; I don't want to harm your father, I want to do him honour. If you don't let us pass my men will kill you,' said Fear Dubh.

'I will not let you pass so long as I'm alive before you,' said Fialan.

The men faced him; and if they did Fialan kept his place, and a battle commenced, the like of which was never seen before that day. Fialan went through the army as a hawk through a flock of sparrows on a March morning, till he killed every man except Fear Dubh. Fear Dubh told him again to leave the ford, he didn't want to harm his father.

'Oh!' said Fialan, 'I know well what you want.'

'If you don't leave that place I'll make you leave it!' said Fear Dubh. Then they closed in combat; and such a combat was never seen before between any two warriors. They made springs to rise through the centre of hard grey rocks, cows to cast their calves whether they had them or not. All the horses of the country were racing about and neighing in dread and fear, and all created things were terrified at the sound and clamour of the fight, till the weapons of Fear Dubh went to pieces in the struggle, and Fialan made two halves of his own sword.

Now they closed in wrestling. In the first round Fialan put Fear Dubh to his knees in the hard bottom of the river; the second round he put him to his hips, and the third, to his shoulders.

'Now,' said he, 'I have you,' giving him a stroke of the half of his sword, which cut the head off him.

Then Fialan went to the door of the castle and told his father what he had done.

Fin chewed his thumb again, and knew what other danger was coming. 'My son,' said he to Fialan, 'Fear Dubh has a younger brother more powerful than he was; that brother is coming against us now with greater forces than those which you have destroyed.'

As soon as Fialan heard these words he hurried to the ford, and waited till the second army came up. He destroyed this army as he had the other, and closed with the second brother in a fight fiercer and more terrible than the first; but at last he thrust him to his armpits in the hard bottom of the river and cut off his head.

Then he went to the castle, and told his father what he had done. A third time Fin chewed his thumb, and said: 'My son, a third army more to be dreaded than the other two is coming now to destroy us, and at the head of it is the youngest brother of Fear Dubh, the most desperate and powerful of the three.'

Again Fialan rushed off to the ford; and, though the work was greater than before, he left not a man of the army alive. Then he closed with the youngest brother of Fear Dubh, and if the first and second battles were terrible this was more terrible by far; but at last he planted the youngest brother up to his armpits in the hard bottom of the river, and swept the head off him.

Now, after the heat and struggle of combat Fialan was in such a rage that he lost his mind from fury, not having any one to fight against; and if the whole world had been there before him he would have gone through it and conquered it all.

But having no one to face him he rushed along the river-bank, tearing the flesh from his own body. Never had such madness been seen in any created being before that day.

Diarmuid came now and knocked at the door of the castle, having the dog Bran with him, and asked Fin what had caused him to raise the cry of distress.

'Oh, Diarmuid,' said Fin, 'we are all fastened in here to be killed. Fialan has destroyed three armies, and Fear Dubh with his two brothers. He is raging now along the bank of the river; you must not go near him, for he would tear you limb from limb. At this moment he wouldn't spare me, his own father; but after a while he will cease from raging and die down; then you can go. The mother of Fear Dubh is coming, and will soon be at the ford. She is more violent, more venomous, more to be dreaded, a greater warrior than her sons. The chief weapon she has are the nails on her fingers; each nail is seven perches long, of the hardest steel on earth. She is coming in the air at this moment with the speed of a hawk, and she has a kŭŕan (a small vessel), with liquor in it, which has such power that if she puts three drops of it on the mouths of her sons they will rise up as well as ever; and if she brings them to life there is nothing to save us.

'Go to the ford; she will be hovering over the corpses of the three armies to know can she find her sons, and as soon as she sees them she will dart down and give them the liquor. You must rise with a mighty bound upon her, dash the kŭŕan out of her hand and spill the liquor.

'If you can kill her save her blood, for nothing in the world can free us from this place and open the door of the castle but the blood of the old hag. I'm in dread you'll not succeed, for she is far more terrible than all her sons together. Go now; Fialan is dying away, and the old woman is coming; make no delay.'

Diarmuid hurried to the ford, stood watching a while; then he saw high in the air something no larger than a hawk. As it came nearer and nearer he saw it was the old woman. She hovered high in the air over the ford. At last she saw her sons, and was swooping down, when Diarmuid rose with a bound into the air and struck the vial a league out of her hand.

The old hag gave a shriek that was heard to the eastern world, and screamed: 'Who has dared to interfere with me or my sons?'

'I,' answered Diarmuid; 'and you'll not go further till I do to you what has been done to your sons.'

The fight began; and if there ever was a fight, before or since, it could not be more terrible than this one; but great as was the power of Diarmuid he never could have conquered but for Bran the dog.

The old woman with her nails stripped the skin and flesh from Diarmuid almost to the vitals. But Bran tore the skin and flesh off the old woman's back from her head to her heels.

From the dint of blood-loss and fighting, Diarmuid was growing faint. Despair came on him, and he was on the point of giving way, when a little robin flew near to him, and sitting on a bush, spoke, saying:

'Oh, Diarmuid, take strength; rise and sweep the head off the old hag, or Fin and the Fenians of Erin are no more.'

Diarmuid took courage, and with his last strength made one great effort, swept the head off the old hag and caught her blood in a vessel. He rubbed some on his own wounds – they were cured; then he cured Bran.

Straightway he took the blood to the castle, rubbed drops of it on the door, which opened, and he went in.

All laughed with joy at the rescue. He freed Fin and his men by rubbing the blood on the chairs; but when he came as far as Conan Maol the blood gave out.

All were going away. 'Why should you leave me here after you,' cried Conan Maol, 'I would rather die at once than stay here for a lingering death. Why don't you, Oscar, and you, Gol MacMorna, come and tear me out of this place; anyhow you'll be able to drag the arms out of me and kill me at once; better that than leave me to die alone.'

Oscar and Gol took each a hand, braced their feet against his feet, put forth all their strength and brought him standing; but if they did, he left all the skin and much of the flesh from the back of his head to his heels on the floor behind him. He was covered with blood, and by all accounts was in a terrible condition, bleeding and wounded.

Now there were sheep grazing near the castle. The Fenians ran out, killed and skinned the largest and best of the flock, and clapped the fresh skin on Conan's back; and such was the healing power in the sheep, and the wound very fresh, that Conan's back healed, and he marched home with the rest of the men, and soon got well; and if he did, they sheared off his back wool enough every year to make a pair of stockings for each one of the Fenians of Erin, and for Fin himself.

And that was a great thing to do and useful, for wool was scarce in Erin in those days. Fin and his men lived pleasantly and joyously for some time; and if they didn't, may we.

THE THREE DAUGHTERS OF KING O'HARA

By Jeremiah Curtin

T here was a king in Desmond whose name was Coluath O'Hara, and he had three daughters. On a time when the king was away from home, the eldest daughter took a thought that she'd like to be married. So she went up in the castle, put on the cloak of darkness which her father had, and wished for the most beautiful man under the sun as a husband for herself.

She got her wish; for scarcely had she put off the cloak of darkness, when there came, in a golden coach with four horses, two black and two white, the finest man she had ever laid eyes on, and took her away.

When the second daughter saw what had happened to her sister, she put on the cloak of darkness, and wished for the next best man in the world as a husband.

She put off the cloak; and straightway there came, in a golden coach with four black horses, a man nearly as good as the first, and took her away.

The third sister put on the cloak, and wished for the best white dog in the world.

Presently he came, with one man attending, in a golden coach and four snow-white horses, and took the youngest sister away.

When the king came home, the stable-boy told him what had happened while he was gone. He was enraged beyond measure when he heard that his youngest daughter had wished for a white dog, and gone off with him.

When the first man brought his wife home he asked: 'In what form will you have me in the daytime – as I am now in the daytime, or as I am now at night?'

'As you are now in the daytime.'

So the first sister had her husband as a man in the daytime; but at night he was a seal.

The second man put the same question to the middle sister, and got the same answer; so the second sister had her husband in the same form as the first.

When the third sister came to where the white dog lived, he asked her: 'How will you have me to be in the daytime – as I am now in the day, or as I am now at night?'

'As you are now in the day.'

So the white dog was a dog in the daytime, but the most beautiful of men at night.

After a time the third sister had a son; and one day, when her husband was going out to hunt, he warned her that if anything should happen to the child, not to shed a tear on that account.

While he was gone, a great grey crow that used to haunt the place came and carried the child away when it was a week old.

Remembering the warning, she shed not a tear for the loss.

All went on as before till another son was born. The husband used to go hunting every day, and again he said she must not shed a tear if anything happened.

When the child was a week old a great grey crow came and bore him away; but the mother did not cry or drop a tear.

All went well till a daughter was born. When she was a week old a great grey crow came and swept her away. This time the mother dropped one tear on a handkerchief, which she took out of her pocket, and then put back again.

When the husband came home from hunting and heard what the crow had done, he asked the wife, 'Have you shed tears this time?'

'I have dropped one tear,' said she.

Then he was very angry; for he knew what harm she had done by dropping that one tear.

Soon after their father invited the three sisters to visit him and be present at a great feast in their honour. They sent messages, each from her own place, that they would come.

The king was very glad at the prospect of seeing his children; but the queen was grieved, and thought it a great disgrace that her youngest daughter had no one to come home with her but a white dog.

The white dog was in dread that the king wouldn't leave him inside with the company, but would drive him from the castle to the yard, and that the dogs outside wouldn't leave a patch of skin on his back, but would tear the life out of him.

The youngest daughter comforted him. 'There is no danger to you,' said she, 'for wherever I am, you'll be, and wherever you go, I'll follow and take care of you.'

When all was ready for the feast at the castle, and the company were assembled, the king was for banishing the white dog; but the youngest daughter would not listen to her father – would not let the white dog out of her sight, but kept him near her at the feast, and divided with him the food that came to herself.

When the feast was over, and all the guests had gone, the three sisters went to their own rooms in the castle.

Late in the evening the queen took the cook with her, and stole in to see what was in her daughters' rooms. They were all asleep at the time. What should she see by the side of her youngest daughter but the most beautiful man she had ever laid eyes on.

Then she went to where the other two daughters were sleeping; and there, instead of the two men who brought them to the feast, were two seals, fast asleep.

The queen was greatly troubled at the sight of the seals. When she and the cook were returning, they came upon the skin of the white dog. She caught it up as she went, and threw it into the kitchen fire.

The skin was not five minutes in the fire when it gave a crack that woke not only all in the castle, but all in the country for miles around.

The husband of the youngest daughter sprang up. He was very angry and very sorry, and said: 'If I had been able to spend three nights with you under your father's roof, I should have got back my own form again for good, and could have been a man both in the day and the night; but now I must go.'

He rose from the bed, ran out of the castle, and away he went as fast as ever his two legs could carry him, overtaking the one before him, and leaving the one behind. He was this way all that night and

the next day; but he couldn't leave the wife, for she followed from the castle, was after him in the night and the day too, and never lost sight of him.

In the afternoon he turned, and told her to go back to her father; but she would not listen to him. At nightfall they came to the first house they had seen since leaving the castle. He turned and said: 'Do you go inside and stay in this house till morning; I'll pass the night outside where I am.'

The wife went in. The woman of the house rose up, gave her a pleasant welcome, and put a good supper before her. She was not long in the house when a little boy came to her knee and called her 'Mother.'

The woman of the house told the child to go back to his place, and not to come out again.

'Here are a pair of scissors,' said the woman of the house to the king's daughter, 'and they will serve you well. Whatever ragged people you see, if you cut a piece off their rags, that moment they will have new clothes of cloth of gold.'

She stayed that night, for she had good welcome. Next morning when she went out, her husband said: 'You'd better go home now to your father.'

'I'll not go to my father if I have to leave you,' said she.

So he went on, and she followed. It was that way all the day till night came; and at nightfall they saw another house at the foot of a hill, and again the husband stopped and said: 'You go in; I'll stop outside till morning.'

The woman of the house gave her a good welcome. After she had eaten and drunk, a little boy came out of another room, ran to her

knee, and said, 'Mother.' The woman of the house sent the boy back
to where he had come from, and told him to stay there.

Next morning, when the princess was going out to her husband,
the woman of the house gave her a comb, and said: 'If you meet
any person with a diseased and a sore head, and draw this comb
over it three times, the head will be well, and covered with the most
beautiful golden hair ever seen.'

She took the comb, and went out to her husband.

'Leave me now,' said he, 'and go back to your own father.'

'I will not,' said she, 'but I will follow you while I have the power.'
So they went forward that day, as on the other two.

At nightfall they came to a third house, at the foot of a hill,
where the princess received a good welcome. After she had eaten
supper, a little girl with only one eye came to her knee and said,
'Mother.'

The princess began to cry at sight of the child, thinking that she
herself was the cause that it had but one eye. Then she put her hand
into her pocket where she kept the handkerchief on which she had
dropped the tear when the grey crow carried her infant away. She
had never used the handkerchief since that day, for there was an eye
on it.

She opened the handkerchief, and put the eye in the girl's head. It
grew into the socket that minute, and the child saw out of it as well
as out of the other eye; and then the woman of the house sent the
little one to bed.

Next morning, as the king's daughter was going out, the woman
of the house gave her a whistle, and said: 'Whenever you put this
whistle to your mouth and blow on it, all the birds of the air will

come to you from every quarter under the sun. Be careful of the whistle, as it may serve you greatly.'

'Go back to your father's castle,' said the husband when she came to him, 'for I must leave you to-day.'

They went on together a few hundred yards, and then sat on a green hillock, and he told the wife: 'Your mother has come between us; but for her we might have lived together all our days. If I had been allowed to pass three nights with you in your father's house, I should have got back my form of a man both in the daytime and the night. The Queen of Tir na n-Og (the land of youth) enchanted and put on me a spell, that unless I could spend three nights with a wife under her father's roof in Erin, I should bear the form of a white dog one half of my time; but if the skin of the dog should be burned before the three nights were over, I must go down to her kingdom and marry the queen herself. And 'tis to her I am going to-day. I have no power to stay, and I must leave you; so farewell, you'll never see me again on the upper earth.'

He left her sitting on the mound, went a few steps forward to some bulrushes, pulled up one, and disappeared in the opening where the rush had been.

She stopped there, sitting on the mound lamenting, till evening, not knowing what to do. At last she bethought herself, and going to the rushes, pulled up a stalk, went down, followed her husband, and never stopped till she came to the lower land.

After a while she reached a small house near a splendid castle. She went into the house and asked, could she stay there till morning. 'You can,' said the woman of the house, 'and welcome.'

Next day the woman of the house was washing clothes, for that was how she made a living. The princess fell to and helped her with the work. In the course of that day the Queen of Tir na n-Og and the husband of the princess were married.

Near the castle, and not far from the washerwoman's, lived a henwife with two ragged little daughters. One of them came around the washerwoman's house to play. The child looked so poor and her clothes were so torn and dirty that the princess took pity on her, and cut the clothes with the scissors which she had.

That moment the most beautiful dress of cloth of gold ever seen on woman or child in that kingdom was on the henwife's daughter.

When she saw what she had on, the child ran home to her mother as fast as ever she could go.

'Who gave you that dress?' asked the henwife.

'A strange woman that is in that house beyond,' said the little girl, pointing to the washerwoman's house.

The henwife went straight to the Queen of Tir na n-Og and said: 'There is a strange woman in the place, who will be likely to take your husband from you, unless you banish her away or do something to her; for she has a pair of scissors different from anything ever seen or heard of in this country.'

When the queen heard this she sent word to the princess that, unless the scissors were given up to her without delay, she would have the head off her.

The princess said she would give up the scissors if the queen would let her pass one night with her husband.

The queen answered that she was willing to give her the one night. The princess came and gave up the scissors, and went to her own husband; but the queen had given him a drink, and he

fell asleep, and never woke till after the princess had gone in the morning.

Next day another daughter of the henwife went to the washerwoman's house to play. She was wretched-looking, her head being covered with scabs and sores.

The princess drew the comb three times over the child's head, cured it, and covered it with beautiful golden hair. The little girl ran home and told her mother how the strange woman had drawn the comb over her head, cured it, and given her beautiful golden hair.

The henwife hurried off to the queen and said: 'That strange woman has a comb with wonderful power to cure, and give golden hair; and she'll take your husband from you unless you banish her or take her life.'

The queen sent word to the princess that unless she gave up the comb, she would have her life.

The princess returned as answer that she would give up the comb if she might pass one night with the queen's husband.

The queen was willing, and gave her husband a draught as before. When the princess came, he was fast asleep, and did not waken till after she had gone in the morning.

On the third day the washerwoman and the princess went out to walk, and the first daughter of the henwife with them. When they were outside the town, the princess put the whistle to her mouth and blew. That moment the birds of the air flew to her from every direction in flocks. Among them was a bird of song and new tales. The princess went to one side with the bird. 'What means can I take,' asked she, 'against the queen to get back my husband? Is it best to kill her, and can I do it?'

'It is very hard,' said the bird, 'to kill her. There is no one in all Tir na n-Og who is able to take her life but her own husband. Inside a holly-tree in front of the castle is a wether, in the wether a duck, in the duck an egg, and in that egg is her heart and life. No man in Tir na n-Og can cut that holly-tree but her husband.'

The princess blew the whistle again. A fox and a hawk came to her. She caught and put them into two boxes, which the washerwoman had with her, and took them to her new home.

When the henwife's daughter went home, she told her mother about the whistle. Away ran the henwife to the queen, and said: 'That strange woman has a whistle that brings together all the birds of the air, and she'll have your husband yet, unless you take her head.'

'I'll take the whistle from her, anyhow,' said the queen. So she sent for the whistle.

The princess gave answer that she would give up the whistle if she might pass one night with the queen's husband.

The queen agreed, and gave him a draught as on the other nights. He was asleep when the princess came and when she went away.

Before going, the princess left a letter with his servant for the queen's husband, in which she told how she had followed him to Tir na n-Og, and had given the scissors, the comb, and the whistle, to pass three nights in his company, but had not spoken to him because the queen had given him sleeping draughts; that the life of the queen was in an egg, the egg in a duck, the duck in a wether, the wether in a holly-tree in front of the castle, and that no man could split the tree but himself.

As soon as he got the letter the husband took an axe, and went to the holly-tree. When he came to the tree he found the princess

there before him, having the two boxes with the fox and the hawk in them.

He struck the tree a few blows; it split open, and out sprang the wether. He ran scarce twenty perches before the fox caught him. The fox tore him open; then the duck flew out. The duck had not flown fifteen perches when the hawk caught and killed her, smashing the egg. That instant the Queen of Tir na n-Og died.

The husband kissed and embraced his faithful wife. He gave a great feast; and when the feast was over, he burned the henwife with her house, built a palace for the washerwoman, and made his servant secretary.

They never left Tir na n-Og, and are living there happily now; and so may we live here.

THE WEAVER'S SON AND THE GIANT OF THE WHITE HILL

By Jeremiah Curtin

There was once a weaver in Erin who lived at the edge of a wood; and on a time when he had nothing to burn, he went out with his daughter to get fagots for the fire.

They gathered two bundles, and were ready to carry them home, when who should come along but a splendid-looking stranger on horseback. And he said to the weaver: 'My good man, will you give me that girl of yours?'

'Indeed then I will not,' said the weaver.

'I'll give you her weight in gold,' said the stranger, and he put out the gold there on the ground.

So the weaver went home with the gold and without the daughter. He buried the gold in the garden, without letting his wife know what he had done. When she asked, 'Where is our daughter?' the weaver said: 'I sent her on an errand to a neighbour's house for things that I want.'

Night came, but no sight of the girl. The next time he went for fagots, the weaver took his second daughter to the wood; and when they had two bundles gathered, and were ready to go home, a second stranger came on horseback, much finer than the first, and asked the weaver would he give him his daughter.

'I will not,' said the weaver.

'Well,' said the stranger, 'I'll give you her weight in silver if you'll let her go with me;' and he put the silver down before him.

The weaver carried home the silver and buried it in the garden with the gold, and the daughter went away with the man on horseback.

When he went again to the wood, the weaver took his third daughter with him; and when they were ready to go home, a third man came on horseback, gave the weight of the third daughter in copper, and took her away. The weaver buried the copper with the gold and silver.

Now, the wife was lamenting and moaning night and day for her three daughters, and gave the weaver no rest till he told the whole story.

Now, a son was born to them; and when the boy grew up and was going to school, he heard how his three sisters had been carried away for their weight in gold and silver and copper; and every day when he came home he saw how his mother was lamenting and wandering outside in grief through the fields and pits and ditches, so he asked her what trouble was on her; but she wouldn't tell him a word.

At last he came home crying from school one day, and said: 'I'll not sleep three nights in one house till I find my three sisters.' Then he said to his mother: 'Make me three loaves of bread, mother, for I am going on a journey.'

Next day he asked had she the bread ready. She said she had, and she was crying bitterly all the time. 'I'm going to leave you now, mother,' said he; 'and I'll come back when I have found my three sisters.'

He went away, and walked on till he was tired and hungry; and then he sat down to eat the bread that his mother had given him, when a red-haired man came up and asked him for something to eat. 'Sit down here,' said the boy. He sat down, and the two ate till there was not a crumb of the bread left.

The boy told of the journey he was on; then the red-haired man said: 'There may not be much use in your going, but here are three things that'll serve you – the sword of sharpness, the cloth of plenty, and the cloak of darkness. No man can kill you while that sword is in your hand; and whenever you are hungry or dry, all you have to do is to spread the cloth and ask for what you'd like to eat or drink, and it will be there before you. When you put on the cloak, there won't be a man or a woman or a living thing in the world that'll see you, and you'll go to whatever place you have set your mind on quicker than any wind.'

The red-haired man went his way, and the boy travelled on. Before evening a great shower came, and he ran for shelter to a large oak-tree. When he got near the tree his foot slipped, the ground opened, and down he went through the earth till he came to another country. When he was in the other country he put on the cloak of darkness and went ahead like a blast of wind, and never stopped till he saw a castle in the distance; and soon he was there. But he found nine gates closed before him, and no way to go through. It was written inside the cloak of darkness that his eldest sister lived in that castle.

He was not long at the gate looking in when a girl came to him and said, 'Go on out of that; if you don't, you'll be killed.'

'Do you go in,' said he to the girl, 'and tell my sister, the woman of this castle, to come out to me.' The girl ran in; out came the sister, and asked: 'Why are you here, and what did you come for?'

'I have come to this country to find my three sisters, who were given away by my father for their weight in gold, silver, and copper; and you are my eldest sister.'

She knew from what he said that he was her brother, so she opened the gates and brought him in, saying: 'Don't wonder at anything you see in this castle. My husband is enchanted. I see him only at night. He goes off every morning, stays away all day, and comes home in the evening.'

The sun went down; and while they were talking, the husband rushed in, and the noise of him was terrible. He came in the form of a ram, ran upstairs, and soon after came down a man.

'Who is this that's with you?' asked he of the wife.

'Oh! that's my brother, who has come from Erin to see me,' said she.

Next morning, when the man of the castle was going off in the form of a ram, he turned to the boy and asked, 'Will you stay a few days in my castle? You are welcome.'

'Nothing would please me better,' said the boy; 'but I have made a vow never to sleep three nights in one house till I have found my three sisters.'

'Well,' said the ram, 'since you must go, here is something for you.' And pulling out a bit of his own wool, he gave it to the boy, saying: 'Keep this; and whenever a trouble is on you, take it out, and call on what rams are in the world to help you.' Away went the ram. The boy took farewell of his sister, put on the cloak of darkness, and disappeared. He travelled till hungry and tired, then he sat down, took off the cloak of darkness, spread the cloth of plenty, and asked for meat and drink. After he had eaten and drunk his fill, he took up the cloth, put on the cloak of darkness, and went ahead, passing every wind that was before him, and leaving every wind that was behind.

About an hour before sunset he saw the castle in which his second sister lived. When he reached the gate, a girl came out to him and said: 'Go away from that gate, or you'll be killed.'

'I'll not leave this till my sister who lives in the castle comes out and speaks to me.'

The girl ran in, and out came the sister. When she heard his story and his father's name, she knew that he was her brother, and said: 'Come into the castle, but think nothing of what you'll see or hear. I don't see my husband from morning till night. He goes and comes in a strange form, but he is a man at night.'

About sunset there was a terrible noise, and in rushed the man of the castle in the form of a tremendous salmon. He went flapping upstairs; but he wasn't long there till he came down a fine-looking man.

'Who is that with you?' asked he of the wife. 'I thought you would let no one into the castle while I was gone.'

'Oh! this is my brother, who has come to see me,' said she.

'If he's your brother, he's welcome,' said the man.

They supped, and then slept till morning. When the man of the castle was going out again, in the form of a great salmon, he turned to the boy and said: 'You'd better stay here with us a while.'

'I cannot,' said the boy. 'I made a vow never to sleep three nights in one house till I had seen my three sisters. I must go on now and find my third sister.'

The salmon then took off a piece of his fin and gave it to the boy, saying: 'If any difficulty meets you, or trouble comes on you, call on what salmons are in the sea to come and help you.'

They parted. The boy put on his cloak of darkness, and away he went, more swiftly than any wind. He never stopped till he was hungry and thirsty. Then he sat down, took off his cloak of darkness, spread the cloth of plenty, and ate his fill; when he had eaten, he went on again till near sundown, when he saw the castle where his third sister lived. All three castles were near the sea. Neither sister knew what place she was in, and neither knew where the other two were living.

The third sister took her brother in just as the first and second had done, telling him not to wonder at anything he saw.

They were not long inside when a roaring noise was heard, and in came the greatest eagle that ever was seen. The eagle hurried upstairs, and soon came down a man.

'Who is that stranger there with you?' asked he of the wife. (He, as well as the ram and salmon, knew the boy; he only wanted to try his wife.)

'This is my brother, who has come to see me.'

They all took supper and slept that night. When the eagle was going away in the morning, he pulled a feather out of his wing, and said to the boy: 'Keep this; it may serve you. If you are ever in straits and want help, call on what eagles are in the world, and they'll come to you.'

There was no hurry now, for the third sister was found; and the boy went upstairs with her to examine the country all around, and to look at the sea. Soon he saw a great white hill, and on the top of the hill a castle.

'In that castle on the white hill beyond,' said the sister, 'lives a giant, who stole from her home the most beautiful young woman in the world. From all parts the greatest heroes and champions and kings' sons are coming to take her away from the giant and marry her. There is not a man of them all who is able to conquer the giant and free the young woman; but the giant conquers them, cuts their heads off, and then eats their flesh. When he has picked the bones clean, he throws them out; and the whole place around the castle is white with the bones of the men that the giant has eaten.'

'I must go,' said the boy, 'to that castle to know can I kill the giant and bring away the young woman.'

So he took leave of his sister, put on the cloak of darkness, took his sword with him, and was soon inside the castle. The giant was fighting with champions outside. When the boy saw the young woman he took off the cloak of darkness and spoke to her.

'Oh!' said she, 'what can you do against the giant? No man has ever come to this castle without losing his life. The giant kills every man; and no one has ever come here so big that the giant did not eat him at one meal.'

'And is there no way to kill him?' asked the boy.

'I think not,' said she.

'Well, if you'll give me something to eat, I'll stay here; and when the giant comes in, I'll do my best to kill him. But don't let on that I am here.'

Then he put on the cloak of darkness, and no one could see him. When the giant came in, he had the bodies of two men on his back. He threw down the bodies and told the young woman to get them ready for his dinner. Then he snuffed around, and said: 'There's some one here; I smell the blood of an Erineach.'

'I don't think you do,' said the young woman; 'I can't see any one.'

'Neither can I,' said the giant; 'but I smell a man.'

With that the boy drew his sword; and when the giant was struck, he ran in the direction of the blow to give one back; then he was struck on the other side.

They were at one another this way, the giant and the boy with the cloak of darkness on him, till the giant had fifty wounds, and was covered with blood. Every minute he was getting a slash of a sword, but never could give one back. At last he called out: 'Whoever you are, wait till to-morrow, and I'll face you then.'

So the fighting stopped; and the young woman began to cry and lament as if her heart would break when she saw the state the giant was in. 'Oh! you'll be with me no longer; you'll be killed now: what can I do alone without you?' and she tried to please him, and washed his wounds.

'Don't be afraid,' said the giant; 'this one, whoever he is, will not kill me, for there is no man in the world that can kill me.' Then the giant went to bed, and was well in the morning.

Next day the giant and the boy began in the middle of the forenoon, and fought till the middle of the afternoon. The giant was covered with wounds, and he had not given one blow to the boy, and could not see him, for he was always in his cloak of darkness. So the giant had to ask for rest till next morning.

While the young woman was washing and dressing the wounds of the giant she cried and lamented all the time, saying: 'What'll become of me now? I'm afraid you'll be killed this time; and how can I live here without you?'

'Have no fear for me,' said the giant; 'I'll put your mind at rest. In the bottom of the sea is a chest locked and bound, in that chest is a duck, in the duck an egg; and I never can be killed unless some one gets the egg from the duck in the chest at the bottom of the sea, and rubs it on the mole that is under my right breast.'

While the giant was telling this to the woman to put her mind at rest, who should be listening to the story but the boy in the cloak of darkness. The minute he heard of the chest in the sea, he thought of the salmons. So off he hurried to the seashore, which was not far away. Then he took out the fin that his eldest sister's husband had given him, and called on what salmons were in the sea to bring up the chest with the duck inside, and put it out on the beach before him.

He had not long to wait till he saw nothing but salmon – the whole sea was covered with them, moving to land; and they put the chest out on the beach before him.

But the chest was locked and strong; how could he open it? He thought of the rams; and taking out the lock of wool, said: 'I want what rams are in the world to come and break open this chest!'

That minute the rams of the world were running to the seashore, each with a terrible pair of horns on him; and soon they battered the chest to splinters. Out flew the duck, and away she went over the sea.

The boy took out the feather, and said: 'I want what eagles are in the world to get me the egg from that duck.'

That minute the duck was surrounded by the eagles of the world, and the egg was soon brought to the boy. He put the feather, the wool, and the fin in his pocket, put on the cloak of darkness, and went to the castle on the white hill, and told the young woman, when she was dressing the wounds of the giant again, to raise up his arm.

Next day they fought till the middle of the afternoon. The giant was almost cut to pieces, and called for a cessation.

The young woman hurried to dress the wounds, and he said: 'I see you would help me if you could: you are not able. But never fear, I shall not be killed.' Then she raised his arm to wash away the blood, and the boy, who was there in his cloak of darkness, struck the mole with the egg. The giant died that minute.

The boy took the young woman to the castle of his third sister. Next day he went back for the treasures of the giant, and there was more gold in the castle than one horse could draw.

They spent nine days in the castle of the eagle with the third sister. Then the boy gave back the feather, and the two went on till they came to the castle of the salmon, where they spent nine more days with the second sister; and he gave back the fin.

When they came to the castle of the ram, they spent fifteen days with the first sister, and had great feasting and enjoyment. Then the boy gave back the lock of wool to the ram, and taking farewell of his sister and her husband, set out for home with the young woman of the white castle, who was now his wife, bringing presents from the three daughters to their father and mother.

At last they reached the opening near the tree, came up through the ground, and went on to where he met the red-haired man. Then he spread the cloth of plenty, asked for every good meat and drink, and called the red-haired man. He came. The three sat down, ate and drank with enjoyment.

When they had finished, the boy gave back to the red-haired man the cloak of darkness, the sword of sharpness, and the cloth of plenty, and thanked him.

'You were kind to me,' said the red-haired man; 'you gave me of your bread when I asked for it, and told me where you were going. I took pity on you; for I knew you never could get what you wanted unless I helped you. I am the brother of the eagle, the salmon, and the ram.'

They parted. The boy went home, built a castle with the treasure of the giant, and lived happily with his parents and wife.

FAIR, BROWN
AND TREMBLING

By Jeremiah Curtin

King Aedh Curucha lived in Tir Conal, and he had three daughters, whose names were Fair, Brown, and Trembling.

Fair and Brown had new dresses, and went to church every Sunday. Trembling was kept at home to do the cooking and work. They would not let her go out of the house at all; for she was more beautiful than the other two, and they were in dread she might marry before themselves.

They carried on in this way for seven years. At the end of seven years the son of the king of Omanya[3] fell in love with the eldest sister.

One Sunday morning, after the other two had gone to church, the old henwife came into the kitchen to Trembling, and said: 'It's at church you ought to be this day, instead of working here at home.'

---

[3] The ancient Emania in Ulster.

'How could I go?' said Trembling. 'I have no clothes good enough to wear at church; and if my sisters were to see me there, they'd kill me for going out of the house.'

'I'll give you,' said the henwife, 'a finer dress than either of them has ever seen. And now tell me what dress will you have?'

'I'll have,' said Trembling, 'a dress as white as snow, and green shoes for my feet.'

Then the henwife put on the cloak of darkness, clipped a piece from the old clothes the young woman had on, and asked for the whitest robes in the world and the most beautiful that could be found, and a pair of green shoes.

That moment she had the robe and the shoes, and she brought them to Trembling, who put them on. When Trembling was dressed and ready, the henwife said: 'I have a honey-bird here to sit on your right shoulder, and a honey-finger to put on your left. At the door stands a milk-white mare, with a golden saddle for you to sit on, and a golden bridle to hold in your hand.'

Trembling sat on the golden saddle; and when she was ready to start, the henwife said: 'You must not go inside the door of the church, and the minute the people rise up at the end of Mass, do you make off, and ride home as fast as the mare will carry you.'

When Trembling came to the door of the church there was no one inside who could get a glimpse of her but was striving to know who she was; and when they saw her hurrying away at the end of Mass, they ran out to overtake her. But no use in their running; she was away before any man could come near her. From the minute she left the church till she got home, she overtook the wind before her, and outstripped the wind behind.

She came down at the door, went in, and found the henwife had dinner ready. She put off the white robes, and had on her old dress in a twinkling.

When the two sisters came home the henwife asked: 'Have you any news to-day from the church?'

'We have great news,' said they. 'We saw a wonderful, grand lady at the church-door. The like of the robes she had we have never seen on a woman before. It's little that was thought of our dresses beside what she had on; and there wasn't a man at the church, from the king to the beggar, but was trying to look at her and know who she was.'

The sisters would give no peace till they had two dresses like the robes of the strange lady; but honey-birds and honey-fingers were not to be found.

Next Sunday the two sisters went to church again, and left the youngest at home to cook the dinner.

After they had gone, the henwife came in and asked: 'Will you go to church to-day?'

'I would go,' said Trembling, 'if I could get the going.'

'What robe will you wear?' asked the henwife.

'The finest black satin that can be found, and red shoes for my feet.'

'What colour do you want the mare to be?'

'I want her to be so black and so glossy that I can see myself in her body.'

The henwife put on the cloak of darkness, and asked for the robes and the mare. That moment she had them. When Trembling was dressed, the henwife put the honey-bird on her right shoulder and the honey-finger on her left. The saddle on the mare was silver, and so was the bridle.

When Trembling sat in the saddle and was going away, the henwife ordered her strictly not to go inside the door of the church, but to rush away as soon as the people rose at the end of Mass, and hurry home on the mare before any man could stop her.

That Sunday the people were more astonished than ever, and gazed at her more than the first time; and all they were thinking of was to know who she was. But they had no chance; for the moment the people rose at the end of Mass she slipped from the church, was in the silver saddle, and home before a man could stop her or talk to her.

The henwife had the dinner ready. Trembling took off her satin robe, and had on her old clothes before her sisters got home.

'What news have you to-day?' asked the henwife of the sisters when they came from the church.

'Oh, we saw the grand strange lady again! And it's little that any man could think of our dresses after looking at the robes of satin that she had on! And all at church, from high to low, had their mouths open, gazing at her, and no man was looking at us.'

The two sisters gave neither rest nor peace till they got dresses as nearly like the strange lady's robes as they could find. Of course they were not so good; for the like of those robes could not be found in Erin.

When the third Sunday came, Fair and Brown went to church dressed in black satin. They left Trembling at home to work in the kitchen, and told her to be sure and have dinner ready when they came back.

After they had gone and were out of sight, the henwife came to the kitchen and said: 'Well, my dear, are you for church to-day?'

'I would go if I had a new dress to wear.'

'I'll get you any dress you ask for. What dress would you like?' asked the henwife.

'A dress red as a rose from the waist down, and white as snow from the waist up; a cape of green on my shoulders; and a hat on my head with a red, a white, and a green feather in it; and shoes for my feet with the toes red, the middle white, and the backs and heels green.'

The henwife put on the cloak of darkness, wished for all these things, and had them. When Trembling was dressed, the henwife put the honey-bird on her right shoulder and the honey-finger on her left, and placing the hat on her head, clipped a few hairs from one lock and a few from another with her scissors, and that moment the most beautiful golden hair was flowing down over the girl's shoulders. Then the henwife asked what kind of a mare she would ride. She said white, with blue and gold-coloured diamond-shaped spots all over her body, on her back a saddle of gold, and on her head a golden bridle.

The mare stood there before the door, and a bird sitting between her ears, which began to sing as soon as Trembling was in the saddle, and never stopped till she came home from the church.

The fame of the beautiful strange lady had gone out through the world, and all the princes and great men that were in it came to church that Sunday, each one hoping that it was himself would have her home with him after Mass.

The son of the king of Omanya forgot all about the eldest sister, and remained outside the church, so as to catch the strange lady before she could hurry away.

The church was more crowded than ever before, and there were three times as many outside. There was such a throng before the church that Trembling could only come inside the gate.

As soon as the people were rising at the end of Mass, the lady slipped out through the gate, was in the golden saddle in an instant, and sweeping away ahead of the wind. But if she was, the prince of Omanya was at her side, and, seizing her by the foot, he ran with the mare for thirty perches, and never let go of the beautiful lady till the shoe was pulled from her foot, and he was left behind with it in his hand. She came home as fast as the mare could carry her, and was thinking all the time that the henwife would kill her for losing the shoe.

Seeing her so vexed and so changed in the face, the old woman asked: 'What's the trouble that's on you now?'

'Oh! I've lost one of the shoes off my feet,' said Trembling.

'Don't mind that; don't be vexed,' said the henwife; 'maybe it's the best thing that ever happened to you.'

Then Trembling gave up all the things she had to the henwife, put on her old clothes, and went to work in the kitchen. When the sisters came home, the henwife asked: 'Have you any news from the church?'

'We have indeed,' said they; 'for we saw the grandest sight to-day. The strange lady came again, in grander array than before. On herself and the horse she rode were the finest colors of the world, and between the ears of the horse was a bird which never stopped singing from the time she came till she went away. The lady herself is the most beautiful woman ever seen by man in Erin.'

After Trembling had disappeared from the church, the son of the king of Omanya said to the other kings' sons: 'I will have that lady for my own.'

They all said: 'You didn't win her just by taking the shoe off her foot, you'll have to win her by the point of the sword; you'll have to fight for her with us before you can call her your own.'

'Well,' said the son of the king of Omanya, 'when I find the lady that shoe will fit, I'll fight for her, never fear, before I leave her to any of you.'

Then all the kings' sons were uneasy, and anxious to know who was she that lost the shoe; and they began to travel all over Erin to know could they find her. The prince of Omanya and all the others went in a great company together, and made the round of Erin; they went everywhere – north, south, east, and west. They visited every place where a woman was to be found, and left not a house in the kingdom they did not search, to know could they find the woman the shoe would fit, not caring whether she was rich or poor, of high or low degree.

The prince of Omanya always kept the shoe; and when the young women saw it, they had great hopes, for it was of proper size, neither large nor small, and it would beat any man to know of what material it was made. One thought it would fit her if she cut a little from her great toe; and another, with too short a foot, put something in the tip of her stocking. But no use, they only spoiled their feet, and were curing them for months afterwards.

The two sisters, Fair and Brown, heard that the princes of the world were looking all over Erin for the woman that could wear the shoe, and every day they were talking of trying it on; and one day Trembling spoke up and said: 'Maybe it's my foot that the shoe will fit.'

'Oh, the breaking of the dog's foot on you! Why say so when you were at home every Sunday?' They were that way waiting, and scolding the younger sister, till the princes were near the place. The day they were to come, the sisters put Trembling in a closet, and locked the door on her. When the company came to the house, the prince of Omanya gave the shoe to the sisters. But though they tried and tried, it would fit neither of them.

'Is there any other young woman in the house?' asked the prince.

'There is,' said Trembling, speaking up in the closet; 'I'm here.'

'Oh! we have her for nothing but to put out the ashes,' said the sisters.

But the prince and the others wouldn't leave the house till they had seen her; so the two sisters had to open the door. When Trembling came out, the shoe was given to her, and it fitted exactly.

The prince of Omanya looked at her and said: 'You are the woman the shoe fits, and you are the woman I took the shoe from.'

Then Trembling spoke up, and said: 'Do you stay here till I return.'

Then she went to the henwife's house. The old woman put on the cloak of darkness, got everything for her she had the first Sunday at church, and put her on the white mare in the same fashion. Then Trembling rode along the highway to the front of the house. All who saw her the first time said: 'This is the lady we saw at church.'

Then she went away a second time, and a second time came back on the black mare in the second dress which the henwife gave her. All who saw her the second Sunday said: 'That is the lady we saw at church.'

A third time she asked for a short absence, and soon came back on the third mare and in the third dress. All who saw her the third time said: 'That is the lady we saw at church.' Every man was satisfied, and knew that she was the woman.

Then all the princes and great men spoke up, and said to the son of the king of Omanya: 'You'll have to fight now for her before we let her go with you.'

'I'm here before you, ready for combat,' answered the prince.

Then the son of the king of Lochlin stepped forth. The struggle began, and a terrible struggle it was. They fought for nine hours; and then the son of the king of Lochlin stopped, gave up his claim, and left the field. Next day the son of the king of Spain fought six hours, and yielded his claim. On the third day the son of the king of Nyerfói fought eight hours, and stopped. The fourth day the son of the king of Greece fought six hours, and stopped. On the fifth day no more strange princes wanted to fight; and all the sons of kings in Erin said they would not fight with a man of their own land, that the strangers had had their chance, and as no others came to claim the woman, she belonged of right to the son of the king of Omanya.

The marriage-day was fixed, and the invitations were sent out. The wedding lasted for a year and a day. When the wedding was over, the king's son brought home the bride, and when the time came a son was born. The young woman sent for her eldest sister, Fair, to be with her and care for her. One day, when Trembling was well, and when her husband was away hunting, the two sisters went out to walk; and when they came to the seaside, the eldest pushed the youngest sister in. A great whale came and swallowed her.

The eldest sister came home alone, and the husband asked, 'Where is your sister?'

'She has gone home to her father in Ballyshannon; now that I am well, I don't need her.'

'Well,' said the husband, looking at her, 'I'm in dread, it's my wife that has gone.'

'Oh! no,' said she; 'it's my sister Fair that's gone.'

Since the sisters were very much alike, the prince was in doubt. That night he put his sword between them, and said: 'If you are my wife, this sword will get warm; if not, it will stay cold.'

In the morning when he rose up, the sword was as cold as when he put it there.

It happened when the two sisters were walking by the seashore, that a little cowboy was down by the water minding cattle, and saw Fair push Trembling into the sea; and next day, when the tide came in, he saw the whale swim up and throw her out on the sand. When she was on the sand she said to the cowboy: 'When you go home in the evening with the cows, tell the master that my sister Fair pushed me into the sea yesterday; that a whale swallowed me, and then threw me out, but will come again and swallow me with the coming of the next tide; then he'll go out with the tide, and come again with to-morrow's tide, and throw me again on the strand. The whale will cast me out three times. I'm under the enchantment of this whale, and cannot leave the beach or escape myself. Unless my husband saves me before I'm swallowed the fourth time, I shall be lost. He must come and shoot the whale with a silver bullet when he turns on the broad of his back. Under the breast-fin of the whale is a reddish-

brown spot. My husband must hit him in that spot, for it is the only place in which he can be killed.'

When the cowboy got home, the eldest sister gave him a draught of oblivion, and he did not tell.

Next day he went again to the sea. The whale came and cast Trembling on shore again. She asked the boy: 'Did you tell the master what I told you to tell him?'

'I did not,' said he; 'I forgot.'

'How did you forget?' asked she.

'The woman of the house gave me a drink that made me forget.'

'Well, don't forget telling him this night; and if she gives you a drink, don't take it from her.'

As soon as the cowboy came home, the eldest sister offered him a drink. He refused to take it till he had delivered his message and told all to the master. The third day the prince went down with his gun and a silver bullet in it. He was not long down when the whale came and threw Trembling upon the beach as the two days before. She had no power to speak to her husband till he had killed the whale. Then the whale went out, turned over once on the broad of his back, and showed the spot for a moment only. That moment the prince fired. He had but the one chance, and a short one at that; but he took it, and hit the spot, and the whale, mad with pain, made the sea all around red with blood, and died.

That minute Trembling was able to speak, and went home with her husband, who sent word to her father what the eldest sister had done. The father came, and told him any death he chose to give her to give it. The prince told the father he would leave her life and death with himself. The father had her put out then on the sea in a barrel, with provisions in it for seven years.

In time Trembling had a second child, a daughter. The prince and she sent the cowboy to school, and trained him up as one of their own children, and said: 'If the little girl that is born to us now lives, no other man in the world will get her but him.'

The cowboy and the prince's daughter lived on till they were married. The mother said to her husband: 'You could not have saved me from the whale but for the little cowboy; on that account I don't grudge him my daughter.'

The son of the king of Omanya and Trembling had fourteen children, and they lived happily till the two died of old age.

CUCÚLIN

By Jeremiah Curtin

There was a king in a land not far from Greece who had two daughters, and the younger was fairer than the elder daughter.

This old king made a match between the king of Greece and his own elder daughter; but he kept the younger one hidden away till after the marriage. Then the younger daughter came forth to view; and when the king of Greece saw her, he wouldn't look at his own wife. Nothing would do him but to get the younger sister and leave the elder at home with her father.

The king wouldn't listen to this, wouldn't agree to the change, so the king of Greece left his wife where she was, went home alone in a terrible rage and collected all his forces to march against the kingdom of his father-in-law.

He soon conquered the king and his army and, so far as he was able, he vexed and tormented him. To do this the more completely, he took from him a rod of Druidic spells, enchantment, and ring of youth which he had, and, striking the elder sister with the rod, he

said: 'You will be a serpent of the sea and live outside there in the bay by the castle.'

Then turning to the younger sister, whose name was Gil an Og, he struck her, and said: 'You'll be a cat while inside this castle, and have your own form only when you are outside the walls.'

After he had done this, the king of Greece went home to his own country, taking with him the rod of enchantment and the ring of youth. The king died in misery and grief, leaving his two daughters spellbound.

Now there was a Druid in that kingdom, and the younger sister went to consult him, and asked: 'Shall I ever be released from the enchantment that's on me now?'

'You will not, unless you find the man to release you; and there is no man in the world to do that but a champion who is now with Fin MacCumhail in Erin.'

'Well, how can I find that man?' asked she.

'I will tell you,' said the Druid. 'Do you make a shirt out of your own hair, take it with you, and never stop till you land in Erin and find Fin and his men; the man that the shirt will fit is the man who will release you.'

She began to make the shirt and worked without stopping till it was finished. Then she went on her journey and never rested till she came to Erin in a ship. She went on shore and inquired where Fin and his men were to be found at that time of the year.

'You will find them at Knock an Ar,' was the answer she got.

She went to Knock an Ar carrying the shirt with her. The first man she met was Conan Maol, and she said to him: 'I have come

to find the man this shirt will fit. From the time one man tries it all must try till I see the man it fits.'

The shirt went from hand to hand till Cucúlin put it on. 'Well,' said she, 'it fits as your own skin.'

Now Gil an Og told Cucúlin all that had happened – how her father had forced her sister to marry the king of Greece, how this king had made war on her father, enchanted her sister and herself, and carried off the rod of enchantment with the ring of youth, and how the old Druid said the man this shirt would fit was the only man in the world who could release them.

Now Gil an Og and Cucúlin went to the ship and sailed across the seas to her country and went to her castle.

'You'll have no one but a cat for company to-night,' said Gil an Og. 'I have the form of a cat inside this castle, but outside I have my own appearance. Your dinner is ready, go in.'

After the dinner Cucúlin went to another room apart, and lay down to rest after the journey. The cat came to his pillow, sat there and purred till he fell asleep and slept soundly till morning.

When he rose up, a basin of water, and everything he needed was before him, and his breakfast ready. He walked out after breakfast; Gil an Og was on the green outside before him and said:

'If you are not willing to free my sister and myself, I shall not urge you; but if you do free us, I shall be glad and thankful. Many kings' sons and champions before you have gone to recover the ring and the rod; but they have never come back.'

'Well, whether I thrive or not, I'll venture,' said Cucúlin.

'I will give you,' said Gil an Og, 'a present such as I have never

given before to any man who ventured out on my behalf; I will give you the speckled boat.'

Cucúlin took leave of Gil an Og and sailed away in the speckled boat to Greece, where he went to the king's court, and challenged him to combat.

The king of Greece gathered his forces and sent them out to chastise Cucúlin. He killed them all to the last man. Then Cucúlin challenged the king a second time.

'I have no one now to fight but myself,' said the king; 'and I don't think it becomes me to go out and meet the like of you.'

'If you don't come out to me,' said Cucúlin, 'I'll go in to you and cut the head off you in your own castle.'

'That's enough of impudence from you, you scoundrel,' said the king of Greece. 'I won't have you come into my castle, but I'll meet you on the open plain.'

The king went out, and they fought till Cucúlin got the better of him, bound him head and heels, and said: 'I'll cut the head off you now unless you give me the ring of youth and the rod of enchantment that you took from the father of Gil an Og.'

'Well, I did carry them away,' said the king, 'but it wouldn't be easy for me now to give them to you or to her; for there was a man who came and carried them away, who could take them from you and from me, and from as many more of us, if they were here.'

'Who was that man?' asked Cucúlin.

'His name,' said the king, 'is Lug[4] Longhand. And if I had known

---

[4] Pronounced 'Loog'.

what you wanted, there would have been no difference between us. I'll tell you how I lost the ring and rod and I'll go with you and show you where Lug Longhand lives. But do you come to my castle. We'll have a good time together.'

They set out next day, and never stopped till they came opposite Lug Longhand castle, and Cucúlin challenged his forces to combat.

'I have no forces,' said Lug, 'but I'll fight you myself.' So the combat began, and they spent the whole day at one another, and neither gained the victory.

The king of Greece himself put up a tent on the green in front of the castle, and prepared everything necessary to eat and drink (there was no one else to do it). After breakfast next day, Cucúlin and Lug began fighting again. The king of Greece looked on as the day before.

They fought the whole day till near evening, when Cucúlin got the upper hand of Lug Longhand and bound him head and heels, saying: 'I'll cut the head off you now unless you give me the rod and the ring that you carried away from the king of Greece.'

'Oh, then,' said Lug, 'it would be hard for me to give them to you or to him; for forces came and took them from me; and they would have taken them from you and from him, if you had been here.'

'Who in the world took them from you?' asked the king of Greece.

'Release me from this bond, and come to my castle, and I'll tell you the whole story,' said Lug Longhand.

Cucúlin released him, and they went to the castle. They got good reception and entertainment from Lug that night, and the following morning as well. He said: 'The ring and the rod were taken from me by the knight of the island of the Flood. This island is surrounded by a chain, and there is a ring of fire seven miles wide between the chain

and the castle. No man can come near the island without breaking the chain, and the moment the chain is broken the fire stops burning at that place; and the instant the fire goes down the knight rushes out and attacks and slays every man that's before him.'

The king of Greece, Cucúlin, and Lug Longhand now sailed on in the speckled boat towards the island of the Flood. On the following morning when the speckled boat struck the chain, she was thrown back three days' sail, and was near being sunk, and would have gone to the bottom of the sea but for her own goodness and strength.

As soon as Cucúlin saw what had happened, he took the oars, rowed on again, and drove the vessel forward with such venom that she cut through the chain and went one third of her length on to dry land. That moment the fire was quenched where the vessel struck, and when the knight of the Island saw the fire go out, he rushed to the shore and met Cucúlin, the king of Greece, and Lug Longhand.

When Cucúlin saw him, he threw aside his weapons, caught him, raised him above his head, hurled him down on the flat of his back, bound him head and heels, and said: 'I'll cut the head off you unless you give me the ring and the rod that you carried away from Lug Longhand.'

'I took them from him, it's true,' said the knight; 'but it would be hard for me to give them to you now; for a man came and took them from me, who would have taken them from you and all that are with you, and as many more if they had been here before him.'

'Who in the world could that man be?' asked Cucúlin.

'The Dark Gruagach of the Northern Island. Release me, and come to my castle. I'll tell you all and entertain you well.'

He took them to his castle, gave them good cheer, and told them all about the Gruagach and his island. Next morning all sailed away in Cucúlin's vessel, which they had left at the shore of the island, and never stopped till they came to the Gruagach's castle, and pitched their tents in front of it.

Then Cucúlin challenged the Gruagach. The others followed after to know would he thrive. The Gruagach came out and faced Cucúlin, and they began and spent the whole day at one another and neither of them gained the upper hand. When evening came, they stopped and prepared for supper and the night.

Next day after breakfast Cucúlin challenged the Gruagach again, and they fought till evening; when Cucúlin got the better in the struggle, disarmed the Gruagach, bound him, and said: 'Unless you give up the rod of enchantment and the ring of youth that you took from the knight of the island of the Flood, I'll cut the head off you now.'

'I took them from him, 'tis true; but there was a man named Thin-in-Iron, who took them from me, and he would have taken them from you and from me, and all that are here, if there were twice as many. He is such a man that sword cannot cut him, fire cannot burn him, water cannot drown him, and 'tis no easy thing to get the better of him. But if you'll free me now and come to my castle, I'll treat you well and tell you all about him.' Cucúlin agreed to this.

Next morning they would not stop nor be satisfied till they went their way. They found the castle of Thin-in-Iron, and Cucúlin challenged him to combat. They fought; and he was cutting the flesh from Cucúlin, but Cucúlin's sword cut no flesh from him. They fought till Cucúlin said: 'It is time now to stop till to-morrow.'

Cucúlin was scarcely able to reach the tent. They had to support him and put him to bed. Now, who should come to Cucúlin that night but Gil an Og, and she said: 'You have gone further than any man before you, and I'll cure you now, and you need go no further for the rod of enchantment and the ring of youth.'

'Well,' said Cucúlin, 'I'll never give over till I knock another day's trial out of Thin-in-Iron.'

When it was time for rest, Gil an Og went away, and Cucúlin fell asleep for himself. On the following morning all his comrades were up and facing his tent. They thought to see him dead, but he was in as good health as ever.

They prepared breakfast, and after breakfast Cucúlin went before the door of the castle to challenge his enemy.

Thin-in-Iron thrust his head out and said: 'That man I fought yesterday has come again to-day. It would have been a good deed if I had cut the head off him last night. Then he wouldn't be here to trouble me this morning. I won't come home this day till I bring his head with me. Then I'll have peace.'

They met in combat and fought till the night was coming. Then Thin-in-Iron cried out for a cessation, and if he did, Cucúlin was glad to give it; for his sword had no effect upon Thin-in-Iron except to tire and nearly kill him (he was enchanted and no arms could cut him). When Thin-in-Iron went to his castle, he threw up three sups of blood, and said to his housekeeper: 'Though his sword could not penetrate me, he has nearly broken my heart.'

Cucúlin had to be carried to his tent. His comrades laid him on his bed and said: 'Whoever came and healed him yesterday, may be the same will be here to-night.' They went away and were not long

gone when Gil an Og came and said: 'Cucúlin, if you had done my bidding, you wouldn't be as you are to-night. But if you neglect my words now, you'll never see my face again. I'll cure you this time and make you as well as ever;' and whatever virtue she had she healed him so he was as strong as before.

'Oh, then,' said Cucúlin, 'whatever comes on me I'll never turn back till I knock another day's trial out of Thin-in-Iron.'

'Well,' said she, 'you are a stronger man than he, but there is no good in working at him with a sword. Throw your sword aside to-morrow, and you'll get the better of him and bind him. You'll not see me again.'

She went away and he fell asleep. His comrades came in the morning and found him sleeping. They got breakfast, and, after eating, Cucúlin went out and called a challenge.

'Oh, 'tis the same man as yesterday,' said Thin-in-Iron, 'and if I had cut the head off him then, it wouldn't be he that would trouble me to-day. If I live for it, I'll bring his head in my hand to-night, and he'll never disturb me again.'

When Cucúlin saw Thin-in-Iron coming, he threw his sword aside, and facing him, caught him by the body, raised him up, then dashed him to the ground, and said, 'If you don't give me what I want, I'll cut the head off you.'

'What do you want of me?' asked Thin-in-Iron.

'I want the rod of enchantment and the ring of youth you carried from the Gruagach.'

'I did indeed carry them from him, but it would be no easy thing for me to give them to you or any other man; for a force came which took them from me.'

'What could take them from you?' asked Cucúlin.

'The queen of the Wilderness, an old hag that has them now. But release me from this bondage and I'll take you to my castle and entertain you well, and I'll go with you and the rest of the company to see how will you thrive.'

So he took Cucúlin and his friends to the castle and entertained them joyously, and he said: 'The old hag, the queen of the Wilderness, lives in a round tower, which is always turning on wheels. There is but one entrance to the tower, and that high above the ground, and in the one chamber in which she lives, keeping the ring and the rod, is a chair, and she has but to sit on the chair and wish herself in any part of the world, and that moment she is there. She has six lines of guards protecting her tower, and if you pass all of these, you'll do what no man before you has done to this day. The first guards are two lions that rush out to know which of them will get the first bite out of the throat of any one that tries to pass. The second are seven men with iron hurlies and an iron ball, and with their hurlies they wallop the life out of any man that goes their way. The third is Hung-up-Naked, who hangs on a tree with his toes to the earth, his head cut from his shoulders and lying on the ground, and who kills every man who comes near him. The fourth is the bull of the Mist that darkens the woods for seven miles around, and destroys everything that enters the Mist. The fifth are seven cats with poison tails; and one drop of their poison would kill the strongest man.'

Next morning all went with Cucúlin as far as the lions who guarded the queen of the Wilderness, an old hag made young by the ring of youth. The two lions ran at Cucúlin to see which would have the first bite out of him.

Cucúlin wore a red silk scarf around his neck and had a fine head of hair. He cut the hair off his head and wound it around one hand, took his scarf and wrapped it around the other. Then rushing at the lions, he thrust a hand down the throat of each lion (for lions can bite neither silk nor hair). He pulled the livers and lights out of the two and they fell dead before him. His comrades looking on, said: 'You'll thrive now since you have done this deed;' and they left him and went home, each to his own country.

Cucúlin went further. The next people he met were the seven men with the iron hurlies (ball clubs), and they said; ''Tis long since any man walked this way to us; we'll have sport now.'

The first one said: 'Give him a touch of the hurly and let the others do the same; and we'll wallop him till he is dead.'

Now Cucúlin drew his sword and cut the head off the first man before he could make an offer of the hurly at him; and then he did the same to the other six.

He went on his way till he came to Hung-up-Naked, who was hanging from a tree, his head on the ground near him. The queen of the Wilderness had fastened him to the tree because he wouldn't marry her; and she said: 'If any man comes who will put your head on you, you'll be free.' And she laid the injunction on him to kill every man who tried to pass his way without putting the head on him.

Cucúlin went up, looked at him, and saw heaps of bones around the tree. The body said: 'You can't go by here. I fight with every man who tries to pass.'

'Well, I'm not going to fight with a man unless he has a head on him. Take your head.' And Cucúlin, picking up the head, clapped it on the body, and said, 'Now I'll fight with you!'

The man said: 'I'm all right now. I know where you are going. I'll stay here till you come; if you conquer you'll not forget me. Take the head off me now; put it where you found it; and if you succeed, remember that I shall be here before you on your way home.'

Cucúlin went on, but soon met the bull of the Mist that covered seven miles of the wood with thick mist. When the bull saw him, he made at him and stuck a horn in his ribs and threw him three miles into the wood, against a great oak tree and broke three ribs in his side.

'Well,' said Cucúlin, when he recovered, 'if I get another throw like that, I'll not be good for much exercise.' He was barely on his feet when the bull was at him again; but when he came up he caught the bull by both horns and away they went wrestling and struggling. For three days and nights Cucúlin kept the bull in play, till the morning of the fourth day, when he put him on the flat of his back. Then he turned him on the side, and putting a foot on one horn and taking the other in his two hands, he said: ''Tis well I earned you; there is not a stitch on me that isn't torn to rags from wrestling with you.' He pulled the bull asunder from his horns to his tail, into two equal parts, and said: 'Now that I have you in two, it's in quarters I'll put you.' He took his sword, and when he struck the backbone of the bull, the sword remained in the bone and he couldn't pull it out.

He walked away and stood awhile and looked. ''Tis hard to say,' said he, 'that any good champion would leave his sword behind him.' So he went back and made another pull and took the hilt off his sword, leaving the blade in the back of the bull. Then he went away tattered and torn, the hilt in his hand, and he turned up towards the forge of the Strong Smith. One of the Smith's boys was out for coal at the time: he saw Cucúlin coming with the hilt in his hand, and ran in, saying: 'There is a man coming up and he looks like a fool; we'll have fun!'

'Hold your tongue!' said the master. 'Have you heard any account of the bull of the Mist these three days?'

'We have not,' said the boys.

'Perhaps,' said the Strong Smith, 'that's a good champion that's coming, and do you mind yourselves.'

At that moment Cucúlin walked in to the forge where twelve boys and the master were working. He saluted them and asked, 'Can you put a blade in this hilt?'

'We can,' said the master. They put in the blade. Cucúlin raised the sword and took a shake out of it and broke it to bits.

'This is a rotten blade,' said he. 'Go at it again.'

They made a second blade. The boys were in dread of him now. He broke the second blade in the same way as the first. They made six blades, one stronger than the other. He did the same to them all.'

There is no use in talking,' said the Strong Smith; 'we have no stuff that would make a right blade for you. Go down now,' said he to two of the boys, 'and bring up an old sword that's down in the stable full of rust.'

They went and brought up the sword on two hand-spikes between them; it was so heavy that one couldn't carry it. They gave it to Cucúlin, and with one blow on his heel he knocked the dust from it and went out at the door and took a shake out of it; and if he did, he darkened the whole place with the rust from the blade.

'This is my sword, whoever made it,' said he.

'It is,' said the master; 'it's yours and welcome. I know who you are now, and where you are going. Remember that I'm in bondage here.' The Strong Smith took Cucúlin then to his house, gave him refreshment and clothes for the journey. When he was ready, the Smith said: 'I hope you'll thrive. You have done a deal more than any man that ever walked this way before. There is nothing now to stand in your way till you come to the seven cats outside the turning tower. If they shake their tails and a drop of poison comes on you, it will penetrate to your heart. You must sweep off their tails with your sword. 'Tis equal to you what their bodies will do after that.'

Cucúlin soon came to them and there wasn't one of the seven cats he didn't strip of her tail before she knew he was in it. He cared nothing for the bodies so he had the tails. The cats ran away.

Now he faced the tower turning on wheels. The queen of the Wilderness was in it. He had been told by Thin-in-Iron that he must cut the axle. He found the axle, cut it, and the tower stopped that instant. Cucúlin made a spring and went in through the single passage.

The old hag was preparing to sit on the chair as she saw him coming. He sprang forward, pushed the chair away with one hand, and, catching her by the back of the neck with the other, said: 'You are to lose your head now, old woman!'

'Spare me, and what you want you'll get,' said she. 'I have the ring of youth and the rod of enchantment,' and she gave them to him. He put the ring on his finger, and saying, 'You'll never do mischief again to man!' he turned her face to the entrance, and gave her a kick. Out she flew through the opening and down to the ground, where she broke her neck and died on the spot.

Cucúlin made the Strong Smith king over all the dominions of the queen of the Wilderness, and proclaimed that any person in the country who refused to obey the new king would be put to death.

Cucúlin turned back at once, and travelled till he came to Hung-up-Naked. He took him down, and putting the head on his body, struck him a blow of the rod and made the finest looking man of him that could be found. The man went back to his own home happy and well.

Cucúlin never stopped till he came to the castle of Gil an Og. She was outside with a fine welcome before him; and why not, to be sure, for he had the rod of enchantment and the ring of youth!

When she entered the castle and took the form of a cat, he struck her a blow of the rod and she gained the same form and face she had before the king of Greece struck her. Then he asked, 'Where is your sister?'

'In the lake there outside,' answered Gil an Og, 'in the form of a sea-serpent.' She went out with him, and the moment they came to the edge of the lake the sister rose up near them. Then Cucúlin struck her with the rod and she came to land in her own shape and countenance.

Next day they saw a deal of vessels facing the harbour, and what should they be but a fleet of ships, and on the ships were the king of Greece, Lug Longhand, the knight of the island of the Flood, the Dark Gruagach of the Northern Island and Thin-in-Iron: and they came each in his own vessel to know was there any account of Cucúlin. There was good welcome for them all, and when they had feasted and rejoiced together Cucúlin married Gil an Og. The king of Greece took Gil an Og's sister, who was his own wife at first, and went home.

Cucúlin went away himself with his wife Gil an Og, never

stopping till he came to Erin; and when he came, Fin MacCumhail and his men were at KilConaly, near the river Shannon.

When Cucúlin went from Erin he left a son whose mother was called the Virago of Alba: she was still alive and the son was eighteen years old. When she heard that Cucúlin had brought Gil an Og to Erin, she was enraged with jealousy and madness. She had reared the son, whose name was Conlán, like any king's son, and now giving him his arms of a champion she told him to go to his father.

'I would,' said he, 'if I knew who my father is.'

'His name is Cucúlin, and he is with Fin MacCumhail. I bind you not to yield to any man,' said she to her son, 'nor tell your name to any man till you fight him out.'

Conlán started from Ulster where his mother was, and never stopped till he was facing Fin and his men, who were hunting that day along the cliffs of KilConaly.

When the young man came up Fin said, 'There is a single man facing us.'

Conan Maol said, 'Let some one go against him, ask who he is and what he wants.'

'I never give an account of myself to any man,' said Conlán, ''till I get an account from him.'

'There is no man among us,' said Conan, 'bound in that way but Cucúlin.' They called on Cucúlin; he came up and the two fought. Conlán knew by the description his mother had given that Cucúlin was his father, but Cucúlin did not know his son. Every time Conlán aimed his spear he threw it so as to strike the ground in front of Cucúlin's toe, but Cucúlin aimed straight at him.

They were at one another three days and three nights. The son

always sparing the father, the father never sparing the son.

Conan Maol came to them the fourth morning. 'Cucúlin,' said he, 'I didn't expect to see any man standing against you three days, and you such a champion.'

When Conlán heard Conan Maol urging the father to kill him, he gave a bitter look at Conan, and forgot his guard. Cucúlin's spear went through his head that minute, and he fell. 'I die of that blow from my father,' said he.

'Are you my son?' said Cucúlin.

'I am,' said Conlán.

Cucúlin took his sword and cut the head off him sooner than leave him in the punishment and pain he was in. Then he faced all the people, and Fin was looking on.

'There's trouble on Cucúlin,' said Fin. 'Chew your thumb,' said Conan Maol, 'to know what's on him.'

Fin chewed his thumb, and said, 'Cucúlin is after killing his own son, and if I and all my men were to face him before his passion cools, at the end of seven days, he'd destroy every man of us.'

'Go now,' said Conan, 'and bind him to go down to Bale strand and give seven days' fighting against the waves of the sea, rather than kill us all.'

So Fin bound him to go down. When he went to Bale strand Cucúlin found a great white stone. He grasped his sword in his right hand and cried out: 'If I had the head of the woman who sent her son into peril of death at my hand, I'd split it as I split this stone,' and he made four quarters of the stone. Then he strove with the waves seven days and nights till he fell from hunger and weakness, and the waves went over him.

BECUMA OF THE WHITE SKIN

By James Stephens

CHAPTER I

There are more worlds than one, and in many ways they are unlike each other. But joy and sorrow, or, in other words, good and evil, are not absent in their degree from any of the worlds, for wherever there is life there is action, and action is but the expression of one or other of these qualities.

After this Earth there is the world of the Shí. Beyond it again lies the Many-Coloured Land. Next comes the Land of Wonder, and after that the Land of Promise awaits us. You will cross clay to get into the Shí; you will cross water to attain the Many-Coloured Land; fire must be passed ere the Land of Wonder is attained, but we do not know what will be crossed for the fourth world.

This adventure of Conn the Hundred Fighter and his son Art was by the way of water, and therefore he was more advanced in magic than Fionn was, all of whose adventures were by the path of

clay and into Faery only, but Conn was the High King and so the arch-magician of Ireland.

A council had been called in the Many-Coloured Land to discuss the case of a lady named Becuma Cneisgel, that is, Becuma of the White Skin, the daughter of Eogan Inver. She had run away from her husband Labraid and had taken refuge with Gadiar, one of the sons of Manannán mac Lir, the god of the sea, and the ruler, therefore, of that sphere.

It seems, then, that there is marriage in two other spheres. In the Shí matrimony is recorded as being parallel in every respect with earth-marriage, and the desire which urges to it seems to be as violent and inconstant as it is with us; but in the Many-Coloured Land marriage is but a contemplation of beauty, a brooding and meditation wherein all grosser desire is unknown and children are born to sinless parents.

In the Shí the crime of Becuma would have been lightly considered, and would have received none or but a nominal punishment, but in the second world a horrid gravity attaches to such a lapse, and the retribution meted is implacable and grim. It may be dissolution by fire, and that can note a destruction too final for the mind to contemplate; or it may be banishment from that sphere to a lower and worse one.

This was the fate of Becuma of the White Skin.

One may wonder how, having attained to that sphere, she could have carried with her so strong a memory of the earth. It is certain that she was not a fit person to exist in the Many-Coloured Land, and it is to be feared that she was organized too grossly even for life in the Shí.

She was an earth-woman, and she was banished to the earth.

Word was sent to the Shís of Ireland that this lady should not be permitted to enter any of them; from which it would seem that the ordinances of the Shí come from the higher world, and, it might follow, that the conduct of earth lies in the Shí.

In that way, the gates of her own world and the innumerable doors of Faery being closed against her, Becuma was forced to appear in the world of men.

It is pleasant, however, notwithstanding her terrible crime and her woeful punishment, to think how courageous she was. When she was told her sentence, nay, her doom, she made no outcry, nor did she waste any time in sorrow. She went home and put on her nicest clothes.

She wore a red satin smock, and, over this, a cloak of green silk out of which long fringes of gold swung and sparkled, and she had light sandals of white bronze on her thin shapely feet. She had long soft hair that was yellow as gold, and soft as the curling foam of the sea. Her eyes were wide and clear as water and were grey as a dove's breast. Her teeth were white as snow and of an evenness to marvel at. Her lips were thin and beautifully curved: red lips in truth, red as winter berries and tempting as the fruits of summer. The people who superintended her departure said mournfully that when she was gone there would be no more beauty left in their world.

She stepped into a coracle, it was pushed on the enchanted waters, and it went forward, world within world, until land appeared, and her boat swung in low tide against a rock at the foot of Ben Edair.

So far for her.

CHAPTER II

Conn the Hundred Fighter, Ard-Rí of Ireland, was in the lowest spirits that can be imagined, for his wife was dead. He had been Ard-Rí for nine years, and during his term the corn used to be reaped three times in each year, and there was full and plenty of everything. There are few kings who can boast of more kingly results than he can, but there was sore trouble in store for him.

He had been married to Eithne, the daughter of Brisland Binn, King of Norway, and, next to his subjects, he loved his wife more than all that was lovable in the world. But the term of man and woman, of king or queen, is set in the stars, and there is no escaping Doom for any one; so, when her time came, Eithne died.

Now there were three great burying-places in Ireland – the Brugh of the Boyne in Ulster, over which Angus Og is chief and god; the Shí mound of Cruachan Ahi, where Ethal Anbual presides over the underworld of Connacht; and Taillltin, in Royal Meath. It was in this last, the sacred place of his own lordship, that Conn laid his wife to rest.

Her funeral games were played during nine days. Her keen was sung by poets and harpers, and a cairn ten acres wide was heaved over her clay. Then the keening ceased and the games drew to an end; the princes of the Five Provinces returned by horse or by chariot to their own places; the concourse of mourners melted away, and there was nothing left by the great cairn but the sun that dozed upon it in the daytime, the heavy clouds that brooded on it in the night, and the desolate, memoried king.

For the dead queen had been so lovely that Conn could not forget her; she had been so kind at every moment that he could not but miss her at every moment; but it was in the Council Chamber and the Judgement Hall that he most pondered her memory. For she had also been wise, and lacking her guidance, all grave affairs seemed graver, shadowing each day and going with him to the pillow at night.

The trouble of the king becomes the trouble of the subject, for how shall we live if judgement is withheld, or if faulty decisions are promulgated? Therefore, with the sorrow of the king, all Ireland was in grief, and it was the wish of every person that he should marry again.

Such an idea, however, did not occur to him, for he could not conceive how any woman should fill the place his queen had vacated. He grew more and more despondent, and less and less fitted to cope with affairs of state, and one day he instructed his son Art to take the rule during his absence, and he set out for Ben Edair.

For a great wish had come upon him to walk beside the sea; to listen to the roll and boom of long, grey breakers; to gaze on an unfruitful, desolate wilderness of waters; and to forget in those sights all that he could forget, and if he could not forget then to remember all that he should remember.

He was thus gazing and brooding when one day he observed a coracle drawing to the shore. A young girl stepped from it and walked to him among black boulders and patches of yellow sand.

CHAPTER III

Being a king he had authority to ask questions. Conn asked her, therefore, all the questions that he could think of, for it is not every day that a lady drives from the sea, and she wearing a golden-

fringed cloak of green silk through which a red satin smock peeped at the openings. She replied to his questions, but she did not tell him all the truth; for, indeed, she could not afford to.

She knew who he was, for she retained some of the powers proper to the worlds she had left, and as he looked on her soft yellow hair and on her thin red lips, Conn recognized, as all men do, that one who is lovely must also be good, and so he did not frame any inquiry on that count; for everything is forgotten in the presence of a pretty woman, and a magician can be bewitched also.

She told Conn that the fame of his son Art had reached even the Many-Coloured Land, and that she had fallen in love with the boy. This did not seem unreasonable to one who had himself ventured much in Faery, and who had known so many of the people of that world leave their own land for the love of a mortal.

'What is your name, my sweet lady?' said the king.

'I am called Delvcaem (Fair Shape) and I am the daughter of Morgan,' she replied.

'I have heard much of Morgan,' said the king. 'He is a very great magician.'

During this conversation Conn had been regarding her with the minute freedom which is right only in a king. At what precise instant he forgot his dead consort we do not know, but it is certain that at this moment his mind was no longer burdened with that dear and lovely memory. His voice was melancholy when he spoke again.

'You love my son!'

'Who could avoid loving him?' she murmured.

'When a woman speaks to a man about the love she feels for another man she is not liked. And,' he continued, 'when she speaks to a man who has no wife of his own about her love for another man then she is disliked.'

'I would not be disliked by you,' Becuma murmured.

'Nevertheless,' said he regally, 'I will not come between a woman and her choice.'

'I did not know you lacked a wife,' said Becuma; but indeed she did.

'You know it now,' the king replied sternly.

'What shall I do?' she inquired; 'Am I to wed you or your son?'

'You must choose,' Conn answered.

'If you allow me to choose it means that you do not want me very badly,' said she with a smile.

'Then I will not allow you to choose,' cried the king, 'and it is with myself you shall marry.'

He took her hand in his and kissed it.

'Lovely is this pale thin hand. Lovely is the slender foot that I see in a small bronze shoe,' said the king.

After a suitable time she continued:

'I should not like your son to be at Tara when I am there, or for a year afterwards, for I do not wish to meet him until I have forgotten him and have come to know you well.'

'I do not wish to banish my son,' the king protested.

'It would not really be a banishment,' she said. 'A prince's duty could be set him, and in such an absence he would improve his knowledge both of Ireland and of men. Further,' she continued with downcast eyes, 'when you remember the reason that brought me here you will see that his presence would be an embarrassment to us both, and my presence would be unpleasant to him if he remembers his mother.'

'Nevertheless,' said Conn stubbornly, 'I do not wish to banish my son; it is awkward and unnecessary.'

'For a year only,' she pleaded.

'It is yet,' he continued thoughtfully, 'a reasonable reason that you give and I will do what you ask, but by my hand and word I don't like doing it.'

They set out then briskly and joyfully on the homeward journey, and in due time they reached Tara of the Kings.

CHAPTER IV

It is part of the education of a prince to be a good chess player, and to continually exercise his mind in view of the judgements that he will be called upon to give and the knotty, tortuous, and perplexing matters which will obscure the issues which he must judge. Art, the son of Conn, was sitting at chess with Cromdes, his father's magician.

'Be very careful about the move you are going to make,' said Cromdes.

'*Can* I be careful?' Art inquired. 'Is the move that you are thinking of in my power?'

'It is not,' the other admitted.

'Then I need not be more careful than usual,' Art replied, and he made his move.

'It is a move of banishment,' said Cromdes.

'As I will not banish myself, I suppose my father will do it, but I do not know why he should.'

'Your father will not banish you.'

'Who then?'

'Your mother.'

'My mother is dead.'

'You have a new one,' said the magician.

'Here is news,' said Art. 'I think I shall not love my new mother.'

'You will yet love her better than she loves you,' said Cromdes, meaning thereby that they would hate each other.

While they spoke the king and Becuma entered the palace.

'I had better go to greet my father,' said the young man.

'You had better wait until he sends for you,' his companion advised, and they returned to their game.

In due time a messenger came from the king directing Art to leave Tara instantly, and to leave Ireland for one full year.

He left Tara that night, and for the space of a year he was not seen again in Ireland. But during that period things did not go well with the king nor with Ireland. Every year before that time three crops of corn used to be lifted off the land, but during Art's absence there was no corn in Ireland and there was no milk. The whole land went hungry.

Lean people were in every house, lean cattle in every field; the bushes did not swing out their timely berries or seasonable nuts; the bees went abroad as busily as ever, but each night they returned languidly, with empty pouches, and there was no honey in their hives when the honey season came. People began to look at each other questioningly, meaningly, and dark remarks passed between them, for they knew that a bad harvest means, somehow, a bad king, and, although this belief can be combated, it is too firmly rooted in wisdom to be dismissed.

The poets and magicians met to consider why this disaster should have befallen the country, and by their arts they discovered the truth

about the king's wife, and that she was Becuma of the White Skin, and they discovered also the cause of her banishment from the Many-Coloured Land that is beyond the sea, which is beyond even the grave.

They told the truth to the king, but he could not bear to be parted from that slender-handed, gold-haired, thin-lipped, blithe enchantress, and he required them to discover some means whereby he might retain his wife and his crown. There was a way and the magicians told him of it.

'If the son of a sinless couple can be found and if his blood be mixed with the soil of Tara the blight and ruin will depart from Ireland,' said the magicians.

'If there is such a boy I will find him,' cried the Hundred Fighter.

At the end of a year Art returned to Tara. His father delivered to him the sceptre of Ireland, and he set out on a journey to find the son of a sinless couple such as he had been told of.

CHAPTER V

The High King did not know where exactly he should look for such a saviour, but he was well educated and knew how to look for whatever was lacking. This knowledge will be useful to those upon whom a similar duty should ever devolve.

He went to Ben Edair. He stepped into a coracle and pushed out to the deep, and he permitted the coracle to go as the winds and the waves directed it.

In such a way he voyaged among the small islands of the sea until he lost all knowledge of his course and was adrift far out in ocean. He was under the guidance of the stars and the great luminaries.

He saw black seals that stared and barked and dived dancingly, with the round turn of a bow and the forward onset of an arrow. Great whales came heaving from the green-hued void, blowing a wave of the sea high into the air from their noses and smacking their wide flat tails thunderously on the water. Porpoises went snorting past in bands and clans. Small fish came sliding and flickering, and all the outlandish creatures of the deep rose by his bobbing craft and swirled and sped away.

Wild storms howled by him so that the boat climbed painfully to the sky on a mile-high wave, balanced for a tense moment on its level top, and sped down the glassy side as a stone goes furiously from a sling.

Or, again, caught in the chop of a broken sea, it stayed shuddering and backing, while above his head there was only a low sad sky, and around him the lap and wash of grey waves that were never the same and were never different.

After long staring on the hungry nothingness of air and water he would stare on the skin-stretched fabric of his boat as on a strangeness, or he would examine his hands and the texture of his skin and the stiff black hairs that grew behind his knuckles and sprouted around his ring, and he found in these things newness and wonder.

Then, when days of storm had passed, the low grey clouds shivered and cracked in a thousand places, each grim islet went scudding to the horizon as though terrified by some great breadth, and when they had passed he stared into vast after vast of blue infinity, in the depths of which his eyes stayed and could not pierce, and wherefrom they could scarcely be withdrawn. A sun beamed thence that filled

the air with sparkle and the sea with a thousand lights, and looking on these he was reminded of his home at Tara: of the columns of white and yellow bronze that blazed out sunnily on the sun, and the red and white and yellow painted roofs that beamed at and astonished the eye.

Sailing thus, lost in a succession of days and nights, of winds and calms, he came at last to an island.

His back was turned to it, and long before he saw it he smelled it and wondered; for he had been sitting as in a daze, musing on a change that had seemed to come in his changeless world; and for a long time he could not tell what that was which made a difference on the salt-whipped wind or why he should be excited. For suddenly he had become excited and his heart leaped in violent expectation.

'It is an October smell,' he said.

'It is apples that I smell.'

He turned then and saw the island, fragrant with apple trees, sweet with wells of wine; and, hearkening towards the shore, his ears, dulled yet with the unending rhythms of the sea, distinguished and were filled with song; for the isle was, as it were, a nest of birds, and they sang joyously, sweetly, triumphantly.

He landed on that lovely island, and went forward under the darting birds, under the apple boughs, skirting fragrant lakes about which were woods of the sacred hazel and into which the nuts of knowledge fell and swam; and he blessed the gods of his people because of the ground that did not shiver and because of the deeply rooted trees that could not gad or budge.

CHAPTER VI

Having gone some distance by these pleasant ways he saw a shapely house dozing in the sunlight.

It was thatched with the wings of birds, blue wings and yellow and white wings, and in the centre of the house there was a door of crystal set in posts of bronze.

The queen of this island lived there, Rigru (Large-eyed), the daughter of Lodan, and wife of Daire Degamra. She was seated on a crystal throne with her son Segda by her side, and they welcomed the High King courteously.

There were no servants in this palace; nor was there need for them. The High King found that his hands had washed themselves, and when later on he noticed that food had been placed before him he noticed also that it had come without the assistance of servile hands. A cloak was laid gently about his shoulders, and he was glad of it, for his own was soiled by exposure to sun and wind and water, and was not worthy of a lady's eye.

Then he was invited to eat.

He noticed, however, that food had been set for no one but himself, and this did not please him, for to eat alone was contrary to the hospitable usage of a king, and was contrary also to his contract with the gods.

'Good my hosts,' he remonstrated, 'it is geasa (taboo) for me to eat alone.'

'But we never eat together,' the queen replied.

'I cannot violate my geasa,' said the High King.

'I will eat with you,' said Segda (Sweet Speech), 'and thus, while you are our guest you will not do violence to your vows.'

'Indeed,' said Conn, 'that will be a great satisfaction, for I have already all the trouble that I can cope with and have no wish to add to it by offending the gods.'

'What is your trouble?' the gentle queen asked.

'During a year,' Conn replied, 'there has been neither corn nor milk in Ireland. The land is parched, the trees are withered, the birds do not sing in Ireland, and the bees do not make honey.'

'You are certainly in trouble,' the queen assented.

'But,' she continued, 'for what purpose have you come to our island?'

'I have come to ask for the loan of your son.'

'A loan of my son!'

'I have been informed,' Conn explained, 'that if the son of a sinless couple is brought to Tara and is bathed in the waters of Ireland the land will be delivered from those ills.'

The king of this island, Daire, had not hitherto spoken, but he now did so with astonishment and emphasis.

'We would not lend our son to any one, not even to gain the kingship of the world,' said he.

But Segda, observing that the guest's countenance was dis-composed, broke in:

'It is not kind to refuse a thing that the Ard-Rí of Ireland asks for, and I will go with him.'

'Do not go, my pulse,' his father advised.

'Do not go, my one treasure,' his mother pleaded.

'I must go indeed,' the boy replied, 'for it is to do good I am required, and no person may shirk such a requirement.'

'Go then,' said his father, 'but I will place you under the protection of the High King and of the Four Provincial Kings of Ireland, and under the protection of Art, the son of Conn, and of Fionn, the son of Uail, and under the protection of the magicians and poets and the men of art in Ireland.' And he thereupon bound these protections and safeguards on the Ard-Rí with an oath.

'I will answer for these protections,' said Conn.

He departed then from the island with Segda and in three days they reached Ireland, and in due time they arrived at Tara.

CHAPTER VII

On reaching the palace Conn called his magicians and poets to a council and informed them that he had found the boy they sought – the son of a virgin. These learned people consulted together, and they stated that the young man must be killed, and that his blood should be mixed with the earth of Tara and sprinkled under the withered trees.

When Segda heard this he was astonished and defiant; then, seeing that he was alone and without prospect of succour, he grew downcast and was in great fear for his life. But remembering the safeguards under which he had been placed, he enumerated these to the assembly, and called on the High King to grant him the protections that were his due.

Conn was greatly perturbed, but, as in duty bound, he placed the boy under the various protections that were in his oath, and, with the courage of one who has no more to gain or lose, he placed Segda, furthermore, under the protection of all the men of Ireland.

But the men of Ireland refused to accept that bond, saying that although the Ard-Rí was acting justly towards the boy he was not acting justly towards Ireland.

'We do not wish to slay this prince for our pleasure,' they argued, 'but for the safety of Ireland he must be killed.'

Angry parties were formed. Art, and Fionn the son of Uail, and the princes of the land were outraged at the idea that one who had been placed under their protection should be hurt by any hand. But the men of Ireland and the magicians stated that the king had gone to Faery for a special purpose, and that his acts outside or contrary to that purpose were illegal, and committed no person to obedience.

There were debates in the Council Hall, in the market-place, in the streets of Tara, some holding that national honour dissolved and absolved all personal honour, and others protesting that no man had aught but his personal honour, and that above it not the gods, not even Ireland, could be placed – for it is to be known that Ireland is a god.

Such a debate was in course, and Segda, to whom both sides addressed gentle and courteous arguments, grew more and more disconsolate.

'You shall die for Ireland, dear heart,' said one of them, and he gave Segda three kisses on each cheek.

'Indeed,' said Segda, returning those kisses, 'indeed I had not bargained to die for Ireland, but only to bathe in her waters and to remove her pestilence.'

'But, dear child and prince,' said another, kissing him likewise, 'if any one of us could save Ireland by dying for her how cheerfully we would die.'

And Segda, returning his three kisses, agreed that the death was noble, but that it was not in his undertaking.

Then, observing the stricken countenances about him, and the faces of men and women hewn thin by hunger, his resolution melted away, and he said:

'I think I must die for you,' and then he said:

'I will die for you.'

And when he had said that, all the people present touched his cheek with their lips, and the love and peace of Ireland entered into his soul, so that he was tranquil and proud and happy.

The executioner drew his wide, thin blade and all those present covered their eyes with their cloaks, when a wailing voice called on the executioner to delay yet a moment. The High King uncovered his eyes and saw that a woman had approached driving a cow before her.

'Why are you killing the boy?' she demanded.

The reason for this slaying was explained to her.

'Are you sure,' she asked, 'that the poets and magicians really know everything?'

'Do they not?' the king inquired.

'Do they?' she insisted.

And then turning to the magicians:

'Let one magician of the magicians tell me what is hidden in the bags that are lying across the back of my cow.'

But no magician could tell it, nor did they try to.

'Questions are not answered thus,' they said. 'There are formulae, and the calling up of spirits, and lengthy complicated preparations in our art.'

'I am not badly learned in these arts,' said the woman, 'and I say that if you slay this cow the effect will be the same as if you had killed the boy.'

'We would prefer to kill a cow or a thousand cows rather than harm this young prince,' said Conn, 'but if we spare the boy will these evils return?'

'They will not be banished until you have banished their cause.'

'And what is their cause?'

'Becuma is the cause, and she must be banished.'

'If you must tell me what to do,' said Conn, 'tell me at least to do something that I can do.'

'I will tell you certainly. You can keep Becuma and your ills as long as you want to. It does not matter to me. Come, my son,' she said to Segda, for it was Segda's mother who had come to save him; and then that sinless queen and her son went back to their home of enchantment, leaving the king and Fionn and the magicians and nobles of Ireland astonished and ashamed.

CHAPTER VIII

There are good and evil people in this and in every other world, and the person who goes hence will go to the good or the evil that is native to him, while those who return come as surely to their due. The trouble which had fallen on Becuma did not leave her repentant, and the sweet lady began to do wrong as instantly and innocently as a flower begins to grow. It was she who was responsible for the ills which had come on Ireland, and we may wonder why she brought these plagues and droughts to what was now her own country.

Under all wrong-doing lies personal vanity or the feeling that we are endowed and privileged beyond our fellows. It is probable that, however courageously she had accepted fate, Becuma had been sharply stricken in her pride; in the sense of personal strength, aloofness, and identity, in which the mind likens itself to god and will resist every domination but its own. She had been punished, that is, she had submitted to control, and her sense of freedom, of privilege, of very being, was outraged. The mind flinches even from the control of natural law, and how much more from the despotism of its own separated likenesses, for if another can control me that other has usurped me, has become me, and how terribly I seem diminished by the seeming addition!

This sense of separateness is vanity, and is the bed of all wrong-doing. For we are not freedom, we are control, and we must submit to our own function ere we can exercise it. Even unconsciously we accept the rights of others to all that we have, and if we will not share our good with them, it is because we cannot, having none; but we will yet give what we have, although that be evil. To insist on other people sharing in our personal torment is the first step towards insisting that they shall share in our joy, as we shall insist when we get it.

Becuma considered that if she must suffer all else she met should suffer also. She raged, therefore, against Ireland, and in particular she raged against young Art, her husband's son, and she left undone nothing that could afflict Ireland or the prince. She may have felt that she could not make them suffer, and that is a maddening thought to any woman. Or perhaps she had really desired the son instead of the father, and her thwarted desire had perpetuated itself as hate. But it

is true that Art regarded his mother's successor with intense dislike, and it is true that she actively returned it.

One day Becuma came on the lawn before the palace, and seeing that Art was at chess with Cromdes she walked to the table on which the match was being played and for some time regarded the game. But the young prince did not take any notice of her while she stood by the board, for he knew that this girl was the enemy of Ireland, and he could not bring himself even to look at her.

Becuma, looking down on his beautiful head, smiled as much in rage as in disdain.

'O son of a king,' said she, 'I demand a game with you for stakes.'

Art then raised his head and stood up courteously, but he did not look at her.

'Whatever the queen demands I will do,' said he.

'Am I not your mother also?' she replied mockingly, as she took the seat which the chief magician leaped from.

The game was set then, and her play was so skilful that Art was hard put to counter her moves. But at a point of the game Becuma grew thoughtful, and, as by a lapse of memory, she made a move which gave the victory to her opponent. But she had intended that. She sat then, biting on her lip with her white small teeth and staring angrily at Art.

'What do you demand from me?' she asked.

'I bind you to eat no food in Ireland until you find the wand of Curoi, son of Darè.'

Becuma then put a cloak about her and she went from Tara northward and eastward until she came to the dewy, sparkling Brugh of Angus mac an Og in Ulster, but she was not admitted there. She went thence to the Shí ruled over by Eogabal, and although this lord would not admit her, his daughter Ainè, who was her foster-sister, let her into Faery. She made inquiries and was informed where the dun of Curoi mac Darè was, and when she had received this intelligence she set out for Sliev Mis. By what arts she coaxed Curoi to give up his wand it matters not, enough that she was able to return in triumph to Tara. When she handed the wand to Art, she said:

'I claim my game of revenge.'

'It is due to you,' said Art, and they sat on the lawn before the palace and played.

A hard game that was, and at times each of the combatants sat for an hour staring on the board before the next move was made, and at times they looked from the board and for hours stared on the sky seeking as though in heaven for advice. But Becuma's foster-sister, Ainè, came from the Shí, and, unseen by any, she interfered with Art's play, so that, suddenly, when he looked again on the board, his face went pale, for he saw that the game was lost.

'I didn't move that piece,' said he sternly.

'Nor did I,' Becuma replied, and she called on the onlookers to confirm that statement.

She was smiling to herself secretly, for she had seen what the mortal eyes around could not see.

'I think the game is mine,' she insisted softly.

'I think that your friends in Faery have cheated,' he replied, 'but the game is yours if you are content to win it that way.'

'I bind you,' said Becuma, 'to eat no food in Ireland until you have found Delvcaem, the daughter of Morgan.'

'Where do I look for her?' said Art in despair.

'She is in one of the islands of the sea,' Becuma replied, 'that is all I will tell you,' and she looked at him maliciously, joyously, contentedly, for she thought he would never return from that journey, and that Morgan would see to it.

CHAPTER IX

Art, as his father had done before him, set out for the Many-Coloured Land, but it was from Inver Colpa he embarked and not from Ben Edair.

At a certain time he passed from the rough green ridges of the sea to enchanted waters, and he roamed from island to island asking all people how he might come to Delvcaem, the daughter of Morgan. But he got no news from any one, until he reached an island that was fragrant with wild apples, gay with flowers, and joyous with the song of birds and the deep mellow drumming of the bees. In this island he was met by a lady, Credè, the Truly Beautiful, and when they had exchanged kisses, he told her who he was and on what errand he was bent.

'We have been expecting you,' said Credè, 'but alas, poor soul, it is a hard, and a long, bad way that you must go; for there is sea and land, danger and difficulty between you and the daughter of Morgan.'

'Yet I must go there,' he answered.

'There is a wild dark ocean to be crossed. There is a dense wood where every thorn on every tree is sharp as a spear-point and is curved and clutching. There is a deep gulf to be gone through,' she said, 'a place of silence and terror, full of dumb, venomous monsters.

There is an immense oak forest – dark, dense, thorny, a place to be strayed in, a place to be utterly bewildered and lost in. There is a vast dark wilderness, and therein is a dark house, lonely and full of echoes, and in it there are seven gloomy hags, who are warned already of your coming and are waiting to plunge you in a bath of molten lead.'

'It is not a choice journey,' said Art, 'but I have no choice and must go.'

'Should you pass those hags,' she continued, 'and no one has yet passed them, you must meet Ailill of the Black Teeth, the son of Mongan Tender Blossom, and who could pass that gigantic and terrible fighter?'

'It is not easy to find the daughter of Morgan,' said Art in a melancholy voice.

'It is not easy,' Credè replied eagerly, 'and if you will take my advice – '

'Advise me,' he broke in, 'for in truth there is no man standing in such need of counsel as I do.'

'I would advise you,' said Credè in a low voice, 'to seek no more for the sweet daughter of Morgan, but to stay in this place where all that is lovely is at your service.'

'But, but – ' cried Art in astonishment.

'Am I not as sweet as the daughter of Morgan?' she demanded, and she stood before him queenly and pleadingly, and her eyes took his with imperious tenderness.

'By my hand,' he answered, 'you are sweeter and lovelier than any being under the sun, but – '

'And with me,' she said, 'you will forget Ireland.'

'I am under bonds,' cried Art, 'I have passed my word, and I would not forget Ireland or cut myself from it for all the kingdoms of the Many-Coloured Land.'

Credè urged no more at that time, but as they were parting she whispered, 'There are two girls, sisters of my own, in Morgan's palace. They will come to you with a cup in either hand; one cup will be filled with wine and one with poison. Drink from the right-hand cup, O my dear.'

Art stepped into his coracle, and then, wringing her hands, she made yet an attempt to dissuade him from that drear journey.

'Do not leave me,' she urged. 'Do not affront these dangers. Around the palace of Morgan there is a palisade of copper spikes, and on the top of each spike the head of a man grins and shrivels. There is one spike only which bears no head, and it is for your head that spike is waiting. Do not go there, my love.'

'I must go indeed,' said Art earnestly.

'There is yet a danger,' she called. 'Beware of Delvcaem's mother, Dog Head, daughter of the King of the Dog Heads. Beware of her.'

'Indeed,' said Art to himself, 'there is so much to beware of that I will beware of nothing. I will go about my business,' he said to the waves, 'and I will let those beings and monsters and the people of the Dog Heads go about their business.'

CHAPTER X

He went forward in his light bark, and at some moment found that he had parted from those seas and was adrift on vaster and more turbulent billows. From those dark-green surges there gaped at him monstrous and cavernous jaws; and round, wicked, red-rimmed, bulging eyes stared fixedly at the boat. A ridge of inky water rushed foaming mountainously on his board, and behind that ridge came a vast warty head that gurgled and groaned. But at these vile creatures he thrust with his lengthy spear or stabbed at closer reach with a dagger.

He was not spared one of the terrors which had been foretold. Thus, in the dark thick oak forest he slew the seven hags and buried them in the molten lead which they had heated for him. He climbed an icy mountain, the cold breath of which seemed to slip into his body and chip off inside of his bones, and there, until he mastered the sort of climbing on ice, for each step that he took upwards he slipped back ten steps. Almost his heart gave way before he learned to climb that venomous hill. In a forked glen into which he slipped at nightfall he was surrounded by giant toads, who spat poison, and were icy as the land they lived in, and were cold and foul and savage. At Sliav Saev he encountered the long-maned lions who lie in wait for the beasts of the world, growling woefully as they squat above their prey and crunch those terrified bones. He came on Ailill of the Black Teeth sitting on the bridge that spanned a torrent, and the grim giant was grinding his teeth on a pillar stone. Art drew nigh unobserved and brought him low.

It was not for nothing that these difficulties and dangers were in his path. These things and creatures were the invention of Dog Head, the wife of Morgan, for it had become known to her that she would die on the day her daughter was wooed. Therefore none of the dangers encountered by Art were real, but were magical chimeras conjured against him by the great witch.

Affronting all, conquering all, he came in time to Morgan's dun, a place so lovely that after the miseries through which he had struggled he almost wept to see beauty again.

Delvcaem knew that he was coming. She was waiting for him, yearning for him. To her mind Art was not only love, he was freedom, for the poor girl was a captive in her father's home. A great pillar a hundred feet high had been built on the roof of Morgan's palace, and on the top of this pillar a tiny room had been constructed, and in this room Delvcaem was a prisoner.

She was lovelier in shape than any other princess of the Many-Coloured Land. She was wiser than all the other women of that land, and she was skilful in music, embroidery, and chastity, and in all else that pertained to the knowledge of a queen.

Although Delvcaem's mother wished nothing but ill to Art, she yet treated him with the courtesy proper in a queen on the one hand and fitting towards the son of the King of Ireland on the other. Therefore, when Art entered the palace he was met and kissed, and he was bathed and clothed and fed. Two young girls came to him then, having a cup in each of their hands, and presented him with the kingly drink, but, remembering the warning which Credè had given him, he drank only from the right-hand cup and escaped the poison.

Next he was visited by Delvcaem's mother, Dog Head, daughter of the King of the Dog Heads, and Morgan's queen. She was dressed in full armour, and she challenged Art to fight with her.

It was a woeful combat, for there was no craft or sagacity unknown to her, and Art would infallibly have perished by her hand but that her days were numbered, her star was out, and her time had come. It was her head that rolled on the ground when the combat was over, and it was her head that grinned and shrivelled on the vacant spike which she had reserved for Art's.

Then Art liberated Delvcaem from her prison at the top of the pillar and they were affianced together. But the ceremony had scarcely been completed when the tread of a single man caused the palace to quake and seemed to jar the world.

It was Morgan returning to the palace.

The gloomy king challenged him to combat also, and in his honour Art put on the battle harness which he had brought from Ireland. He wore a breastplate and helmet of gold, a mantle of blue satin swung from his shoulders, his left hand was thrust into the grips of a purple shield, deeply bossed with silver, and in the other hand he held the wide-grooved, blue-hilted sword which had rung so often into fights and combats, and joyous feats and exercises.

Up to this time the trials through which he had passed had seemed so great that they could not easily be added to. But if all those trials had been gathered into one vast calamity they would not equal one half of the rage and catastrophe of his war with Morgan.

For what he could not effect by arms Morgan would endeavour by guile, so that while Art drove at him or parried a crafty blow, the shape of Morgan changed before his eyes, and the monstrous king was having at him in another form, and from a new direction.

It was well for the son of the Ard-Rí that he had been beloved by the poets and magicians of his land, and that they had taught him all that was known of shape-changing and words of power.

He had need of all these.

At times, for the weapon must change with the enemy, they fought with their foreheads as two giant stags, and the crash of their monstrous onslaught rolled and lingered on the air long after their skulls had parted. Then as two lions, long-clawed, deep-mouthed, snarling, with rigid mane, with red-eyed glare, with flashing, sharp-white fangs, they prowled lithely about each other seeking for an opening. And then as two green-ridged, white-topped, broad-swung, overwhelming, vehement billows of the deep, they met and crashed and sank into and rolled away from each other; and the noise of these two waves was as the roar of all ocean when the howl of the tempest is drowned in the league-long fury of the surge.

But when the wife's time has come the husband is doomed. He is required elsewhere by his beloved, and Morgan went to rejoin his queen in the world that comes after the Many-Coloured Land, and his victor shore that knowledgeable head away from its giant shoulders.

He did not tarry in the Many-Coloured Land, for he had nothing further to seek there. He gathered the things which pleased him best from among the treasures of its grisly king, and with Delvcaem by his side they stepped into the coracle.

Then, setting their minds on Ireland, they went there as it were in a flash.

The waves of all the worlds seemed to whirl past them in one huge green cataract. The sound of all these oceans boomed in their ears for one eternal instant. Nothing was for that moment but a vast roar and pour of waters. Thence they swung into a silence equally vast, and so sudden that it was as thunderous in the comparison as was the elemental rage they quitted. For a time they sat panting, staring at each other, holding each other, lest not only their lives but their very souls should be swirled away in the gusty passage of world within world; and then, looking abroad, they saw the small bright waves creaming by the rocks of Ben Edair, and they blessed the power that had guided and protected them, and they blessed the comely land of Ir.

On reaching Tara, Delvcaem, who was more powerful in art and magic than Becuma, ordered the latter to go away, and she did so.

She left the king's side. She came from the midst of the counsellors and magicians. She did not bid farewell to any one. She did not say good-bye to the king as she set out for Ben Edair.

Where she could go to no man knew, for she had been banished from the Many-Coloured Land and could not return there. She was forbidden entry to the Shí by Angus Og, and she could not remain in Ireland. She went to Sasana and she became a queen in that country, and it was she who fostered the rage against the Holy Land which has not ceased to this day.

MONGAN'S FRENZY

By James Stephens

CHAPTER I

The abbot of the Monastery of Moville sent word to the story-tellers of Ireland that when they were in his neighbourhood they should call at the monastery, for he wished to collect and write down the stories which were in danger of being forgotten.

'These things also must be told,' said he.

In particular he wished to gather tales which told of the deeds that had been done before the Gospel came to Ireland.

'For,' said he, 'there are very good tales among those ones, and it would be a pity if the people who come after us should be ignorant of what happened long ago, and of the deeds of their fathers.'

So, whenever a story-teller chanced in that neighbourhood he was directed to the monastery, and there he received a welcome and his fill of all that is good for man.

The abbot's manuscript boxes began to fill up, and he used to regard that growing store with pride and joy. In the evenings, when the days grew short and the light went early, he would call for some one of these manuscripts and have it read to him by candle-light, in order that he might satisfy himself that it was as good as he had judged it to be on the previous hearing.

One day a story-teller came to the monastery, and, like all the others, he was heartily welcomed and given a great deal more than his need.

He said that his name was Cairidè, and that he had a story to tell which could not be bettered among the stories of Ireland.

The abbot's eyes glistened when he heard that. He rubbed his hands together and smiled on his guest.

'What is the name of your story?' he asked.

'It is called "Mongan's Frenzy".'

'I never heard of it before,' cried the abbot joyfully.

'I am the only man that knows it,' Cairidè replied.

'But how does that come about?' the abbot inquired.

'Because it belongs to my family,' the story-teller answered. 'There was a Cairidè of my nation with Mongan when he went into Faery. This Cairidè listened to the story when it was first told. Then he told it to his son, and his son told it to his son, and that son's great-great-grandson's son told it to his son's son, and he told it to my father, and my father told it to me.'

'And you shall tell it to me,' cried the abbot triumphantly.

'I will indeed,' said Cairidè.

Vellum was then brought and quills. The copyists sat at their tables. Ale was placed beside the story-teller, and he told this tale to the abbot.

CHAPTER II

Said Cairidè:

Mongan's wife at that time was Brótiarna, the Flame Lady. She was passionate and fierce, and because the blood would flood suddenly to her cheek, so that she who had seemed a lily became, while you looked upon her, a rose, she was called Flame Lady. She loved Mongan with ecstasy and abandon, and for that also he called her Flame Lady.

But there may have been something of calculation even in her wildest moment, for if she was delighted in her affection she was tormented in it also, as are all those who love the great ones of life and strive to equal themselves where equality is not possible.

For her husband was at once more than himself and less than himself. He was less than himself because he was now Mongan. He was more than himself because he was one who had long disappeared from the world of men. His lament had been sung and his funeral games played many, many years before, and Brótiarna sensed in him secrets, experiences, knowledges in which she could have no part, and for which she was greedily envious.

So she was continually asking him little, simple questions à propos of every kind of thing.

She weighed all that he said on whatever subject, and when he talked in his sleep she listened to his dream.

The knowledge that she gleaned from those listenings tormented her far more than it satisfied her, for the names of other women were continually on his lips, sometimes in terms of dear affection, sometimes in accents of anger or despair, and in his sleep he spoke familiarly of people whom the story-tellers told of, but who had been dead for centuries. Therefore she was perplexed, and became filled with a very rage of curiosity.

Among the names which her husband mentioned there was one which, because of the frequency with which it appeared, and because of the tone of anguish and love and longing in which it was uttered, she thought of oftener than the others: this name was Duv Laca. Although she questioned and cross-questioned Cairidè, her story-teller, she could discover nothing about a lady who had been known as the Dark Lady of the Lake. But one night when Mongan seemed to speak with Duv Laca he mentioned her father as Fiachna Duv mac Demain, and the story-teller said that king had been dead for a vast number of years.

She asked her husband then, boldly, to tell her the story of Duv Laca, and under the influence of their mutual love he promised to tell it to her some time, but each time she reminded him of his promise he became confused, and said that he would tell it some other time.

As time went on the poor Flame Lady grew more and more jealous of Duv Laca, and more and more certain that, if only she could know what had happened, she would get some ease to her tormented heart and some assuagement of her perfectly natural curiosity. Therefore she lost no opportunity of reminding Mongan of his promise, and on each occasion he renewed the promise and put it back to another time.

CHAPTER III

In the year when Ciaran the son of the Carpenter died, the same year when Tuathal Maelgariv was killed and the year when Diarmait

the son of Cerrbel became King of all Ireland, the year 538 of our era in short, it happened that there was a great gathering of the men of Ireland at the Hill of Uisneach in Royal Meath.

In addition to the Council which was being held, there were games and tournaments and brilliant deployments of troops, and universal feastings and enjoyments. The gathering lasted for a week, and on the last day of the week Mongan was moving through the crowd with seven guards, his story-teller Cairidè, and his wife.

It had been a beautiful day, with brilliant sunshine and great sport, but suddenly clouds began to gather in the sky to the west, and others came rushing blackly from the east. When these clouds met the world went dark for a space, and there fell from the sky a shower of hailstones, so large that each man wondered at their size, and so swift and heavy that the women and young people of the host screamed from the pain of the blows they received.

Mongan's men made a roof of their shields, and the hailstones battered on the shields so terribly that even under them they were afraid. They began to move away from the host looking for shelter, and when they had gone apart a little way they turned the edge of a small hill and a knoll of trees, and in the twinkling of an eye they were in fair weather.

One minute they heard the clashing and bashing of the hailstones, the howling of the venomous wind, the screams of women and the uproar of the crowd on the Hill of Uisneach, and the next minute they heard nothing more of those sounds and saw nothing more of these sights, for they had been permitted to go at one step out of the world of men and into the world of Faery.

CHAPTER IV

There is a difference between this world and the world of Faery,
but it is not immediately perceptible. Everything that is here is
there, but the things that are there are better than those that are
here. All things that are bright are there brighter. There is more
gold in the sun and more silver in the moon of that land. There
is more scent in the flowers, more savour in the fruit. There is
more comeliness in the men and more tenderness in the women.
Everything in Faery is better by this one wonderful degree, and it
is by this betterness you will know that you are there if you should
ever happen to get there.

Mongan and his companions stepped from the world of storm
into sunshine and a scented world. The instant they stepped they
stood, bewildered, looking at each other silently, questioningly, and
then with one accord they turned to look back whence they had
come.

There was no storm behind them. The sunlight drowsed there
as it did in front, a peaceful flooding of living gold. They saw the
shapes of the country to which their eyes were accustomed, and
recognized the well-known landmarks, but it seemed that the
distant hills were a trifle higher, and the grass which clothed them
and stretched between was greener, was more velvety: that the trees
were better clothed and had more of peace as they hung over the
quiet ground.

But Mongan knew what had happened, and he smiled with glee
as he watched his astonished companions, and he sniffed that balmy
air as one whose nostrils remembered it.

'You had better come with me,' he said.

'Where are we?' his wife asked.

'Why, we are here,' cried Mongan; 'where else should we be?'

He set off then, and the others followed, staring about them cautiously, and each man keeping a hand on the hilt of his sword.

'Are we in Faery?' the Flame Lady asked.

'We are,' said Mongan.

When they had gone a little distance they came to a grove of ancient trees. Mightily tall and well-grown these trees were, and the trunk of each could not have been spanned by ten broad men. As they went among these quiet giants into the dappled obscurity and silence, their thoughts became grave and all the motions of their minds elevated, as though they must equal in greatness and dignity those ancient and glorious trees. When they passed through the grove they saw a lovely house before them, built of mellow wood and with a roof of bronze – it was like the dwelling of a king, and over the windows of the Sunny Room there was a balcony. There were ladies on this balcony, and when they saw the travellers approaching they sent messengers to welcome them.

Mongan and his companions were then brought into the house, and all was done for them that could be done for honoured guests. Everything within the house was as excellent as all without, and it was inhabited by seven men and seven women, and it was evident that Mongan and these people were well acquainted.

In the evening a feast was prepared, and when they had eaten well there was a banquet. There were seven vats of wine, and as Mongan loved wine he was very happy, and he drank more on that occasion than any one had ever noticed him to drink before.

It was while he was in this condition of glee and expansion that the Flame Lady put her arms about his neck and begged he would tell her the story of Duv Laca, and, being boisterous then and full of good spirits, he agreed to her request, and he prepared to tell the tale.

The seven men and seven women of the Fairy Palace then took their places about him in a half-circle; his own seven guards sat behind them; his wife, the Flame Lady, sat by his side; and at the back of all Cairidè his story-teller sat, listening with all his ears, and remembering every word that was uttered.

CHAPTER V

Said Mongan:

In the days of long ago and the times that have disappeared for ever, there was one Fiachna Finn the son of Baltan, the son of Murchertach, the son of Muredach, the son of Eogan, the son of Neill. He went from his own country when he was young, for he wished to see the land of Lochlann, and he knew that he would be welcomed by the king of that country, for Fiachna's father and Eolgarg's father had done deeds in common and were obliged to each other.

He was welcomed, and he stayed at the Court of Lochlann in great ease and in the midst of pleasures.

It then happened that Eolgarg Mor fell sick and the doctors could not cure him. They sent for other doctors, but they could not cure him, nor could any one say what he was suffering from, beyond that he was wasting visibly before their eyes, and would certainly become a shadow and disappear in air unless he was healed and fattened and made visible.

They sent for more distant doctors, and then for others more distant still, and at last they found a man who claimed that he could make a cure if the king were supplied with the medicine which he would order.

'What medicine is that?' said they all.

'This is the medicine,' said the doctor. 'Find a perfectly white cow with red ears, and boil it down in the lump, and if the king drinks that rendering he will recover.'

Before he had well said it messengers were going from the palace in all directions looking for such a cow. They found lots of cows which were nearly like what they wanted, but it was only by chance they came on the cow which would do the work, and that beast belonged to the most notorious and malicious and cantankerous female in Lochlann, the Black Hag. Now the Black Hag was not only those things that have been said; she was also whiskered and warty and one-eyed and obstreperous, and she was notorious and ill-favoured in many other ways also.

They offered her a cow in the place of her own cow, but she refused to give it. Then they offered a cow for each leg of her cow, but she would not accept that offer unless Fiachna went bail for the payment. He agreed to do so, and they drove the beast away.

On the return journey he was met by messengers who brought news from Ireland. They said that the King of Ulster was dead, and that he, Fiachna Finn, had been elected king in the dead king's place. He at once took ship for Ireland, and found that all he had been told was true, and he took up the government of Ulster.

CHAPTER VI

A year passed, and one day as he was sitting at judgement there came a great noise from without, and this noise was so persistent that the people and suitors were scandalized, and Fiachna at last ordered that the noisy person should be brought before him to be judged. It was done, and to his surprise the person turned out to be the Black Hag.

She blamed him in the court before his people, and complained that he had taken away her cow, and that she had not been paid the four cows he had gone bail for, and she demanded judgement from him and justice.

'If you will consider it to be justice, I will give you twenty cows myself,' said Fiachna.

'I would not take all the cows in Ulster,' she screamed.

'Pronounce judgement yourself,' said the king, 'and if I can do what you demand I will do it.' For he did not like to be in the wrong, and he did not wish that any person should have an unsatisfied claim upon him.

The Black Hag then pronounced judgement, and the king had to fulfil it.

'I have come,' said she, 'from the east to the west; you must come from the west to the east and make war for me, and revenge me on the King of Lochlann.'

Fiachna had to do as she demanded, and, although it was with a heavy heart, he set out in three days' time for Lochlann, and he brought with him ten battalions.

He sent messengers before him to Big Eolgarg warning him of his coming, of his intention, and of the number of troops he was bringing; and when he landed Eolgarg met him with an equal force, and they fought together.

In the first battle three hundred of the men of Lochlann were killed, but in the next battle Eolgarg Mor did not fight fair, for he let some venomous sheep out of a tent, and these attacked the men of Ulster and killed nine hundred of them.

So vast was the slaughter made by these sheep and so great the terror they caused, that no one could stand before them, but by great good luck there was a wood at hand, and the men of Ulster, warriors and princes and charioteers, were forced to climb up the trees, and they roosted among the branches like great birds, while the venomous sheep ranged below bleating terribly and tearing up the ground.

Fiachna Finn was also sitting in a tree, very high up, and he was disconsolate.

'We are disgraced!' said he.

'It is very lucky,' said the man in the branch below, 'that a sheep cannot climb a tree.'

'We are disgraced for ever!' said the King of Ulster.

'If those sheep learn how to climb, we are undone surely,' said the man below.

'I will go down and fight the sheep,' said Fiachna.

But the others would not let the king go.

'It is not right,' they said, 'that you should fight sheep.'

'Some one must fight them,' said Fiachna Finn, 'but no more of my men shall die until I fight myself; for if I am fated to die, I will die and I cannot escape it, and if it is the sheep's fate to die, then die they will; for there is no man can avoid destiny, and there is no sheep can dodge it either.'

'Praise be to god!' said the warrior that was higher up.

'Amen!' said the man who was higher than he, and the rest of the warriors wished good luck to the king.

He started then to climb down the tree with a heavy heart, but while he hung from the last branch and was about to let go, he noticed a tall warrior walking towards him. The king pulled himself up on the branch again and sat dangle-legged on it to see what the warrior would do.

The stranger was a very tall man, dressed in a green cloak with a silver brooch at the shoulder. He had a golden band about his hair and golden sandals on his feet, and he was laughing heartily at the plight of the men of Ireland.

CHAPTER VII

'It is not nice of you to laugh at us,' said Fiachna Finn.

'Who could help laughing at a king hunkering on a branch and his army roosting around him like hens?' said the stranger.

'Nevertheless,' the king replied, 'it would be courteous of you not to laugh at misfortune.'

'We laugh when we can,' commented the stranger, 'and are thankful for the chance.'

'You may come up into the tree,' said Fiachna, 'for I perceive that you are a mannerly person, and I see that some of the venomous sheep are charging in this direction. I would rather protect you,' he

continued, 'than see you killed; for,' said he lamentably, 'I am getting down now to fight the sheep.'

'They will not hurt me,' said the stranger.

'Who are you?' the king asked.

'I am Manannán, the son of Lir.'

Fiachna knew then that the stranger could not be hurt.

'What will you give me if I deliver you from the sheep?' asked Manannán.

'I will give you anything you ask, if I have that thing.'

'I ask the rights of your crown and of your household for one day.'

Fiachna's breath was taken away by that request, and he took a little time to compose himself, then he said mildly:

'I will not have one man of Ireland killed if I can save him. All that I have they give me, all that I have I give to them, and if I must give this also, then I will give this, although it would be easier for me to give my life.'

'That is agreed,' said Manannán.

He had something wrapped in a fold of his cloak, and he unwrapped and produced this thing.

It was a dog.

Now if the sheep were venomous, this dog was more venomous still, for it was fearful to look at. In body it was not large, but its head was of a great size, and the mouth that was shaped in that head was able to open like the lid of a pot. It was not teeth which were in that head, but hooks and fangs and prongs. Dreadful was that mouth to look at, terrible to look into, woeful to think about; and from it, or from the broad, loose nose that waggled above it, there came a sound which no word of man could describe, for it was not a snarl, nor was it a howl, although it was both of these. It was neither a growl nor a grunt, although it was both of these; it was not a yowl nor a groan, although it was both of these: for it was one sound made up of these sounds, and there was in it, too, a whine and a yelp, and a long-drawn snoring noise, and a deep purring noise, and a noise that was like the squeal of a rusty hinge, and there were other noises in it also.

'The gods be praised!' said the man who was in the branch above the king.

'What for this time?' said the king.

'Because that dog cannot climb a tree,' said the man.

And the man on a branch yet above him groaned out, 'Amen!'

'There is nothing to frighten sheep like a dog,' said Manannán, 'and there is nothing to frighten these sheep like this dog.'

He put the dog on the ground then.

'Little dogeen, little treasure,' said he, 'go and kill the sheep.'

And when he said that the dog put an addition and an addendum on to the noise he had been making before, so that the men of Ireland stuck their fingers into their ears and turned the whites of their eyes upwards, and nearly fell off their branches with the fear and the fright which that sound put into them.

It did not take the dog long to do what he had been ordered. He went forward, at first, with a slow waddle, and as the venomous sheep came to meet him in bounces, he then went to meet them in wriggles; so that in a while he went so fast that you could see nothing of him but a head and a wriggle. He dealt with the sheep in this way, a jump and a chop for each, and he never missed his jump and he never missed his chop. When he got his grip he swung

round on it as if it was a hinge. The swing began with the chop, and it ended with the bit loose and the sheep giving its last kick. At the end of ten minutes all the sheep were lying on the ground, and the same bit was out of every sheep, and every sheep was dead.

'You can come down now,' said Manannán.

'That dog can't climb a tree,' said the man in the branch above the king warningly.

'Praise be to the gods!' said the man who was above him.

'Amen!' said the warrior who was higher up than that.

And the man in the next tree said:

'Don't move a hand or a foot until the dog chokes himself to death on the dead meat.'

The dog, however, did not eat a bit of the meat. He trotted to his master, and Manannán took him up and wrapped him in his cloak.

'Now you can come down,' said he.

'I wish that dog was dead!' said the king.

But he swung himself out of the tree all the same, for he did not wish to seem frightened before Manannán.

'You can go now and beat the men of Lochlann,' said Manannán. 'You will be King of Lochlann before nightfall.'

'I wouldn't mind that,' said the king.

'It's no threat,' said Manannán.

The son of Lir turned then and went away in the direction of Ireland to take up his one-day rights, and Fiachna continued his battle with the Lochlannachs.

He beat them before nightfall, and by that victory he became King of Lochlann and King of the Saxons and the Britons.

He gave the Black Hag seven castles with their territories, and he gave her one hundred of every sort of cattle that he had captured. She was satisfied.

Then he went back to Ireland, and after he had been there for some time his wife gave birth to a son.

CHAPTER VIII

'You have not told me one word about Duv Laca,' said the Flame Lady reproachfully.

'I am coming to that,' replied Mongan.

He motioned towards one of the great vats, and wine was brought to him, of which he drank so joyously and so deeply that all people wondered at his thirst, his capacity, and his jovial spirits.

'Now, I will begin again.'

Said Mongan:

There was an attendant in Fiachna Finn's palace who was called An Dáv, and the same night that Fiachna's wife bore a son, the wife of An Dáv gave birth to a son also. This latter child was called mac an Dáv, but the son of Fiachna's wife was named Mongan.

'Ah!' murmured the Flame Lady.

The queen was angry. She said it was unjust and presumptuous that the servant should get a child at the same time that she got one herself, but there was no help for it, because the child was there and could not be obliterated.

Now this also must be told.

There was a neighbouring prince called Fiachna Duv, and he was

the ruler of the Dal Fiatach. For a long time he had been at enmity and spiteful warfare with Fiachna Finn; and to this Fiachna Duv there was born in the same night a daughter, and this girl was named Duv Laca of the White Hand.

'Ah!' cried the Flame Lady.

'You see!' said Mongan, and he drank anew and joyously of the fairy wine.

In order to end the trouble between Fiachna Finn and Fiachna Duv the babies were affianced to each other in the cradle on the day after they were born, and the men of Ireland rejoiced at that deed and at that news. But soon there came dismay and sorrow in the land, for when the little Mongan was three days old his real father, Manannán the son of Lir, appeared in the middle of the palace. He wrapped Mongan in his green cloak and took him away to rear and train in the Land of Promise, which is beyond the sea that is at the other side of the grave.

When Fiachna Duv heard that Mongan, who was affianced to his daughter Duv Laca, had disappeared, he considered that his compact of peace was at an end, and one day he came by surprise and attacked the palace. He killed Fiachna Finn in that battle, and he crowned himself King of Ulster.

The men of Ulster disliked him, and they petitioned Manannán to bring Mongan back, but Manannán would not do this until the boy was sixteen years of age and well reared in the wisdom of the Land of Promise. Then he did bring Mongan back, and by his means peace was made between Mongan and Fiachna Duv, and Mongan was married to his cradle-bride, the young Duv Laca.

CHAPTER IX

One day Mongan and Duv Laca were playing chess in their palace. Mongan had just made a move of skill, and he looked up from the board to see if Duv Laca seemed as discontented as she had a right to be. He saw then over Duv Laca's shoulder a little black-faced, tufty-headed cleric leaning against the door-post inside the room.

'What are you doing there?' said Mongan.

'What are you doing there yourself?' said the little black-faced cleric.

'Indeed, I have a right to be in my own house,' said Mongan.

'Indeed I do not agree with you,' said the cleric.

'Where ought I to be, then?' said Mongan.

'You ought to be at Dun Fiathac avenging the murder of your father,' replied the cleric, 'and you ought to be ashamed of yourself for not having done it long ago. You can play chess with your wife when you have won the right to leisure.'

'But how can I kill my wife's father?' Mongan exclaimed.

'By starting about it at once,' said the cleric.

'Here is a way of talking!' said Mongan.

'I know,' the cleric continued, 'that Duv Laca will not agree with a word I say on this subject, and that she will try to prevent you from doing what you have a right to do, for that is a wife's business, but a man's business is to do what I have just told you; so come with me now and do not wait to think about it, and do not wait to play any more chess. Fiachna Duv has only a small force with him at this moment, and we can burn his palace as he burned your father's palace, and kill him as he killed your father, and crown you

King of Ulster rightfully the way he crowned himself wrongfully as a king.'

'I begin to think that you own a lucky tongue, my black-faced friend,' said Mongan, 'and I will go with you.'

He collected his forces then, and he burned Fiachna Duv's fortress, and he killed Fiachna Duv, and he was crowned King of Ulster.

Then for the first time he felt secure and at liberty to play chess. But he did not know until afterwards that the black-faced, tufty-headed person was his father Manannán, although that was the fact.

There are some who say, however, that Fiachna the Black was killed in the year 624 by the lord of the Scot's Dal Riada, Condad Cerr, at the battle of Ard Carainn; but the people who say this do not know what they are talking about, and they do not care greatly what it is they say.

CHAPTER X

'There is nothing to marvel about in this Duv Laca,' said the Flame Lady scornfully. 'She has got married, and she has been beaten at chess. It has happened before.'

'Let us keep to the story,' said Mongan, and, having taken some few dozen deep draughts of the wine, he became even more jovial than before. Then he recommenced his tale:

It happened on a day that Mongan had need of treasure. He had many presents to make, and he had not as much gold and silver and cattle as was proper for a king. He called his nobles together and discussed what was the best thing to be done, and it was arranged that he should visit the provincial kings and ask boons from them.

He set out at once on his round of visits, and the first province he went to was Leinster.

The King of Leinster at that time was Branduv, the son of Echach. He welcomed Mongan and treated him well, and that night Mongan slept in his palace.

When he awoke in the morning he looked out of a lofty window, and he saw on the sunny lawn before the palace a herd of cows. There were fifty cows in all, for he counted them, and each cow had a calf beside her, and each cow and calf was pure white in colour, and each of them had red ears.

When Mongan saw these cows he fell in love with them as he had never fallen in love with anything before.

He came down from the window and walked on the sunny lawn among the cows, looking at each of them and speaking words of affection and endearment to them all; and while he was thus walking and talking and looking and loving, he noticed that some one was moving beside him. He looked from the cows then, and saw that the King of Leinster was at his side.

'Are you in love with the cows?' Branduv asked him.

'I am,' said Mongan.

'Everybody is,' said the King of Leinster.

'I never saw anything like them,' said Mongan.

'Nobody has,' said the King of Leinster.

'I never saw anything I would rather have than these cows,' said Mongan.

'These,' said the King of Leinster, 'are the most beautiful cows in Ireland, and,' he continued thoughtfully, 'Duv Laca is the most beautiful woman in Ireland.'

'There is no lie in what you say,' said Mongan.

'Is it not a queer thing,' said the King of Leinster, 'that I should have what you want with all your soul, and you should have what I want with all my heart.'

'Queer indeed,' said Mongan, 'but what is it that you do want?'

'Duv Laca, of course,' said the King of Leinster.

'Do you mean,' said Mongan, 'that you would exchange this herd of fifty pure white cows having red ears – '

'And their fifty calves,' said the King of Leinster –

'For Duv Laca, or for any woman in the world?'

'I would,' cried the King of Leinster, and he thumped his knee as he said it.

'Done,' roared Mongan, and the two kings shook hands on the bargain.

Mongan then called some of his own people, and before any more words could be said and before any alteration could be made, he set his men behind the cows and marched home with them to Ulster.

CHAPTER XI

Duv Laca wanted to know where the cows came from, and Mongan told her that the King of Leinster had given them to him. She fell in love with them as Mongan had done, but there was nobody in the world could have avoided loving those cows: such cows they were! such wonders! Mongan and Duv Laca used to play chess together, and then they would go out together to look at the cows, and then they would go in together and would talk to each other about the cows. Everything they did they did together, for they loved to be with each other.

However, a change came.

One morning a great noise of voices and trampling of horses and rattle of armour came about the palace. Mongan looked from the window.

'Who is coming?' asked Duv Laca.

But he did not answer her.

'This noise must announce the visit of a king,' Duv Laca continued.

But Mongan did not say a word.

Duv Laca then went to the window.

'Who is that king?' she asked.

And her husband replied to her then:

'That is the King of Leinster,' said he mournfully.

'Well,' said Duv Laca, surprised, 'is he not welcome?'

'He is welcome indeed,' said Mongan lamentably.

'Let us go out and welcome him properly,' Duv Laca suggested.

'Let us not go near him at all,' said Mongan, 'for he is coming to complete his bargain.'

'What bargain are you talking about?' Duv Laca asked.

But Mongan would not answer that.

'Let us go out,' said he, 'for we must go out.'

Mongan and Duv Laca went out then and welcomed the King of Leinster. They brought him and his chief men into the palace, and water was brought for their baths, and rooms were appointed for them, and everything was done that should be done for guests.

That night there was a feast, and after the feast there was a banquet, and all through the feast and the banquet the King of

Leinster stared at Duv Laca with joy, and sometimes his breast was delivered of great sighs, and at times he moved as though in perturbation of spirit and mental agony.

'There is something wrong with the King of Leinster,' Duv Laca whispered.

'I don't care if there is,' said Mongan.

'You must ask what he wants.'

'But I don't want to know it,' said Mongan.

'Nevertheless, you must ask him,' she insisted.

So Mongan did ask him, and it was in a melancholy voice that he asked it.

'Do you want anything?' said he to the King of Leinster.

'I do indeed,' said Branduv.

'If it is in Ulster I will get it for you,' said Mongan mournfully.

'It is in Ulster,' said Branduv.

Mongan did not want to say anything more then, but the King of Leinster was so intent and everybody else was listening and Duv Laca was nudging his arm, so he said:

'What is it that you do want?'

'I want Duv Laca.'

'I want her too,' said Mongan.

'You made your bargain,' said the King of Leinster, 'my cows and their calves for your Duv Laca, and the man that makes a bargain keeps a bargain.'

'I never before heard,' said Mongan, 'of a man giving away his own wife.'

'Even if you never heard of it before, you must do it now,' said Duv Laca, 'for honour is longer than life.'

Mongan became angry when Duv Laca said that. His face went red as a sunset, and the veins swelled in his neck and his forehead.

'Do you say that?' he cried to Duv Laca.

'I do,' said Duv Laca.

'Let the King of Leinster take her,' said Mongan.

CHAPTER XII

Duv Laca and the King of Leinster went apart then to speak together, and the eye of the king seemed to be as big as a plate, so fevered was it and so enlarged and inflamed by the look of Duv Laca. He was so confounded with joy also that his words got mixed up with his teeth, and Duv Laca did not know exactly what it was he was trying to say, and he did not seem to know himself. But at last he did say something intelligible, and this is what he said:

'I am a very happy man,' said he.

'And I,' said Duv Laca, 'am the happiest woman in the world.'

'Why should you be happy?' the astonished king demanded.

'Listen to me,' she said. 'If you tried to take me away from this place against my own wish, one half of the men of Ulster would be dead before you got me and the other half would be badly wounded in my defence.'

'A bargain is a bargain,' the King of Leinster began.

'But,' she continued, 'they will not prevent my going away, for they all know that I have been in love with you for ages.'

'What have you been in with me for ages?' said the amazed king.

'In love with you,' replied Duv Laca.

'This is news,' said the king, 'and it is good news.'

'But, by my word,' said Duv Laca, 'I will not go with you unless you grant me a boon.'

'All that I have,' cried Branduv, 'and all that everybody has.'

'And you must pass your word and pledge your word that you will do what I ask.'

'I pass it and pledge it,' cried the joyful king.

'Then,' said Duv Laca, 'this is what I bind on you.'

'Light the yoke!' he cried.

'Until one year is up and out you are not to pass the night in any house that I am in.'

'By my head and my hand!' Branduv stammered.

'And if you come into a house where I am during the time and term of that year, you are not to sit down in the chair that I am sitting in.'

'Heavy is my doom!' he groaned.

'But,' said Duv Laca, 'if I am sitting in a chair or a seat you are to sit in a chair that is over against me and opposite to me and at a distance from me.'

'Alas!' said the king, and he smote his hands together, and then he beat them on his head, and then he looked at them and at everything about, and he could not tell what anything was or where anything was, for his mind was clouded and his wits had gone astray.

'Why do you bind these woes on me?' he pleaded.

'I wish to find out if you truly love me.'

'But I do,' said the king. 'I love you madly and dearly, and with all my faculties and members.'

'That is the way I love you,' said Duv Laca. 'We shall have a notable year of courtship and joy. And let us go now,' she continued, 'for I am impatient to be with you.'

'Alas!' said Branduv, as he followed her. 'Alas, alas!' said the King of Leinster.

CHAPTER XIII

'I think,' said the Flame Lady, 'that whoever lost that woman had no reason to be sad.'

Mongan took her chin in his hand and kissed her lips.

'All that you say is lovely, for you are lovely,' said he, 'and you are my delight and the joy of the world.'

Then the attendants brought him wine, and he drank so joyously of that and so deeply, that those who observed him thought he would surely burst and drown them. But he laughed loudly and with enormous delight, until the vessels of gold and silver and bronze chimed mellowly to his peal and the rafters of the house went creaking.

For (said he), Mongan loved Duv Laca of the White Hand better than he loved his life, better than he loved his honour. The kingdoms of the world did not weigh with him beside the string of her shoe. He would not look at a sunset if he could see her. He would not listen to a harp if he could hear her speak, for she was the delight of ages, the gem of time, and the wonder of the world till Doom.

She went to Leinster with the king of that country, and when she had gone Mongan fell grievously sick, so that it did not seem he could ever recover again; and he began to waste and wither, and he began to look like a skeleton, and a bony structure, and a misery.

Now this also must be known.

Duv Laca had a young attendant, who was her foster-sister as well as her servant, and on the day that she got married to Mongan, her

attendant was married to mac an Dáv, who was servant and foster-
brother to Mongan. When Duv Laca went away with the King of
Leinster, her servant, mac an Dáv's wife, went with her, so there were
two wifeless men in Ulster at that time, namely, Mongan the king
and mac an Dáv his servant.

One day as Mongan sat in the sun, brooding lamentably on his
fate, mac an Dáv came to him.

'How are things with you, master?' asked mac an Dáv.

'Bad,' said Mongan.

'It was a poor day brought you off with Manannán to the Land of
Promise,' said his servant.

'Why should you think that?' inquired Mongan.

'Because,' said mac an Dáv, 'you learned nothing in the Land of
Promise except how to eat a lot of food and how to do nothing in a
deal of time.'

'What business is it of yours?' said Mongan angrily.

'It is my business surely,' said mac an Dáv, 'for my wife has gone off
to Leinster with your wife, and she wouldn't have gone if you hadn't
made a bet and a bargain with that accursed king.'

Mac an Dáv began to weep then.

'I didn't make a bargain with any king,' said he, 'and yet my wife
has gone away with one, and it's all because of you.'

'There is no one sorrier for you than I am,' said Mongan.

'There is indeed,' said mac an Dáv, 'for I am sorrier myself.'

Mongan roused himself then.

'You have a claim on me truly,' said he, 'and I will not have any one
with a claim on me that is not satisfied. Go,' he said to mac an Dáv,
'to that fairy place we both know of. You remember the baskets I left

there with the sod from Ireland in one and the sod from Scotland in the other; bring me the baskets and sods.'

'Tell me the why of this?' said his servant.

'The King of Leinster will ask his wizards what I am doing, and this is what I will be doing. I will get on your back with a foot in each of the baskets, and when Branduv asks the wizards where I am they will tell him that I have one leg in Ireland and one leg in Scotland, and as long as they tell him that he will think he need not bother himself about me, and we will go into Leinster that way.'

'No bad way either,' said mac an Dáv.

They set out then.

CHAPTER XIV

It was a long, uneasy journey, for although mac an Dáv was of stout heart and good will, yet no man can carry another on his back from Ulster to Leinster and go quick. Still, if you keep on driving a pig or a story they will get at last to where you wish them to go, and the man who continues putting one foot in front of the other will leave his home behind, and will come at last to the edge of the sea and the end of the world.

When they reached Leinster the feast of Moy Lifé was being held, and they pushed on by forced marches and long stages so as to be in time, and thus they came to the Moy of Cell Camain, and they mixed with the crowd that were going to the feast.

A great and joyous concourse of people streamed about them. There were young men and young girls, and when these were not holding each other's hands it was because their arms were round

each other's necks. There were old, lusty women going by, and when these were not talking together it was because their mouths were mutually filled with apples and meat-pies. There were young warriors with mantles of green and purple and red flying behind them on the breeze, and when these were not looking disdainfully on older soldiers it was because the older soldiers happened at the moment to be looking at them. There were old warriors with yard-long beards flying behind their shoulders like wisps of hay, and when these were not nursing a broken arm or a cracked skull, it was because they were nursing wounds in their stomachs or their legs. There were troops of young women who giggled as long as their breaths lasted and beamed when it gave out. Bands of boys who whispered mysteriously together and pointed with their fingers in every direction at once, and would suddenly begin to run like a herd of stampeded horses. There were men with carts full of roasted meats. Women with little vats full of mead, and others carrying milk and beer. Folk of both sorts with towers swaying on their heads, and they dripping with honey. Children having baskets piled with red apples, and old women who peddled shell-fish and boiled lobsters. There were people who sold twenty kinds of bread, with butter thrown in. Sellers of onions and cheese, and others who supplied spare bits of armour, odd scabbards, spear handles, breastplate-laces. People who cut your hair or told your fortune or gave you a hot bath in a pot. Others who put a shoe on your horse or a piece of embroidery on your mantle; and others, again, who took stains off your sword or dyed your finger-nails or sold you a hound.

It was a great and joyous gathering that was going to the feast.

Mongan and his servant sat against a grassy hedge by the roadside and watched the multitude streaming past.

Just then Mongan glanced to the right whence the people were coming. Then he pulled the hood of his cloak over his ears and over his brow.

'Alas!' said he in a deep and anguished voice.

Mac an Dáv turned to him.

'Is it a pain in your stomach, master?'

'It is not,' said Mongan.

'Well, what made you make that brutal and belching noise?'

'It was a sigh I gave,' said Mongan.

'Whatever it was,' said mac an Dáv, 'what was it?'

'Look down the road on this side and tell me who is coming,' said his master.

'It is a lord with his troop.'

'It is the King of Leinster,' said Mongan.

'The man,' said mac an Dáv in a tone of great pity, 'the man that took away your wife! And,' he roared in a voice of extra-ordinary savagery, 'the man that took away my wife into the bargain, and she not in the bargain.'

'Hush,' said Mongan, for a man who heard his shout stopped to tie a sandal, or to listen.

'Master,' said mac an Dáv as the troop drew abreast and moved past.

'What is it, my good friend?'

'Let me throw a little, small piece of a rock at the King of Leinster.'

'I will not.'

'A little bit only, a small bit about twice the size of my head.'

'I will not let you,' said Mongan.

When the king had gone by mac an Dáv groaned a deep and dejected groan.

'Ocón!' said he. 'Ocón-ío-go-deó!' said he.

The man who had tied his sandal said then:

'Are you in pain, honest man?'

'I am not in pain,' said mac an Dáv.

'Well, what was it that knocked a howl out of you like the yelp of a sick dog, honest man?'

'Go away,' said mac an Dáv, 'go away, you flat-faced, nosy person.'

'There is no politeness left in this country,' said the stranger, and he went away to a certain distance, and from thence he threw a stone at mac an Dáv's nose, and hit it.

CHAPTER XV

The road was now not so crowded as it had been. Minutes would pass and only a few travellers would come, and minutes more would go when nobody was in sight at all.

Then two men came down the road: they were clerics.

'I never saw that kind of uniform before,' said mac an Dáv.

'Even if you didn't,' said Mongan, 'there are plenty of them about. They are men that don't believe in our gods,' said he.

'Do they not, indeed?' said mac an Dáv.

'The rascals!' said he. 'What, what would Manannán say to that?'

'The one in front carrying the big book is Tibraidè, he is the priest of Cell Camain, and he is the chief of those two.'

'Indeed, and indeed!' said mac an Dáv. 'The one behind must be his servant, for he has a load on his back.'

The priests were reading their offices, and mac an Dáv marvelled at that.

'What is it they are doing?' said he.

'They are reading.'

'Indeed, and indeed they are,' said mac an Dáv. 'I can't make out a word of the language except that the man behind says amen, amen, every time the man in front puts a grunt out of him. And they don't like our gods at all!' said mac an Dáv.

'They do not,' said Mongan.

'Play a trick on them, master,' said mac an Dáv.

Mongan agreed to play a trick on the priests.

He looked at them hard for a minute, and then he waved his hand at them.

The two priests stopped, and they stared straight in front of them, and then they looked at each other, and then they looked at the sky. The clerk began to bless himself, and then Tibraidè began to bless himself, and after that they didn't know what to do. For where there had been a road with hedges on each side and fields stretching beyond them, there was now no road, no hedge, no field; but there was a great broad river sweeping across their path; a mighty tumble of yellowy-brown waters, very swift, very savage; churning and billowing and jockeying among rough boulders and islands of stone. It was a water of villainous depth and of detestable wetness; of ugly hurrying and of desolate cavernous sound. At a little to their right there was a thin uncomely bridge that waggled across the torrent.

Tibraidè rubbed his eyes, and then he looked again.

'Do you see what I see?' said he to the clerk.

'I don't know what you see,' said the clerk, 'but what I see I never did see before, and I wish I did not see it now.'

'I was born in this place,' said Tibraidè, 'my father was born here before me, and my grandfather was born here before him, but until this day and this minute I never saw a river here before, and I never heard of one.'

'What will we do at all?' said the clerk. 'What will we do at all?'

'We will be sensible,' said Tibraidè sternly, 'and we will go about our business,' said he. 'If rivers fall out of the sky what has that to do with you, and if there is a river here, which there is, why, thank God, there is a bridge over it too.'

'Would you put a toe on that bridge?' said the clerk.

'What is the bridge for?' said Tibraidè.

Mongan and mac an Dáv followed them.

When they got to the middle of the bridge it broke under them, and they were precipitated into that boiling yellow flood.

Mongan snatched at the book as it fell from Tibraidè's hand.

'Won't you let them drown, master?' asked mac an Dáv.

'No,' said Mongan, 'I'll send them a mile down the stream, and then they can come to land.'

Mongan then took on himself the form of Tibraidè and he turned mac an Dáv into the shape of the clerk.

'My head has gone bald,' said the servant in a whisper.

'That is part of it,' replied Mongan.

'So long as we know!' said mac an Dáv.

They went on then to meet the King of Leinster.

CHAPTER XVI

They met him near the place where the games were played.

'Good my soul, Tibraidè!' cried the King of Leinster, and he gave Mongan a kiss. Mongan kissed him back again.

'Amen, amen,' said mac an Dáv.

'What for?' said the King of Leinster.

And then mac an Dáv began to sneeze, for he didn't know what for.

'It is a long time since I saw you, Tibraidè,' said the king, 'but at this minute I am in great haste and hurry. Go you on before me to the fortress, and you can talk to the queen that you'll find there, she that used to be the King of Ulster's wife. Kevin Cochlach, my charioteer, will go with you, and I will follow you myself in a while.'

The King of Leinster went off then, and Mongan and his servant went with the charioteer and the people.

Mongan read away out of the book, for he found it interesting, and he did not want to talk to the charioteer, and mac an Dáv cried, amen, amen, every time that Mongan took his breath. The people who were going with them said to one another that mac an Dáv was a queer kind of clerk, and that they had never seen any one who had such a mouthful of amens.

But in a while they came to the fortress, and they got into it without any trouble, for Kevin Cochlach, the king's charioteer, brought them in. Then they were led to the room where Duv Laca was, and as he went into that room Mongan shut his eyes, for he did not want to look at Duv Laca while other people might be looking at him.

'Let everybody leave this room, while I am talking to the queen,'

said he; and all the attendants left the room, except one, and she wouldn't go, for she wouldn't leave her mistress.

Then Mongan opened his eyes and he saw Duv Laca, and he made a great bound to her and took her in his arms, and mac an Dáv made a savage and vicious and terrible jump at the attendant, and took her in his arms, and bit her ear and kissed her neck and wept down into her back.

'Go away,' said the girl, 'unhand me, villain,' said she.

'I will not,' said mac an Dáv, 'for I'm your own husband, I'm your own mac, your little mac, your macky-wac-wac.' Then the attendant gave a little squeal, and she bit him on each ear and kissed his neck and wept down into his back, and said that it wasn't true and that it was.

CHAPTER XVII

But they were not alone, although they thought they were. The hag that guarded the jewels was in the room. She sat hunched up against the wall, and as she looked like a bundle of rags they did not notice her. She began to speak then.

'Terrible are the things I see,' said she.

'Terrible are the things I see.'

Mongan and his servant gave a jump of surprise, and their two wives jumped and squealed. Then Mongan puffed out his cheeks till his face looked like a bladder, and he blew a magic breath at the hag, so that she seemed to be surrounded by a fog, and when she looked through that breath everything seemed to be different from what she had thought. Then she began to beg everybody's pardon.

'I had an evil vision,' said she, 'I saw crossways. How sad it is that I should begin to see the sort of things I thought I saw.'

'Sit in this chair, mother,' said Mongan, 'and tell me what you thought you saw,' and he slipped a spike under her, and mac an Dáv pushed her into the seat, and she died on the spike.

Just then there came a knocking at the door. Mac an Dáv opened it, and there was Tibraidè standing outside, and twenty-nine of his men were with him, and they were all laughing.

'A mile was not half enough,' said mac an Dáv reproachfully.

The Chamberlain of the fortress pushed into the room and he stared from one Tibraidè to the other.

'This is a fine growing year,' said he. 'There never was a year when Tibraidès were as plentiful as they are this year. There is a Tibraidè outside and a Tibraidè inside, and who knows but there are some more of them under the bed. The place is crawling with them,' said he.

Mongan pointed at Tibraidè.

'Don't you know who that is?' he cried.

'I know who he says he is,' said the Chamberlain.

'Well, he is Mongan,' said Mongan, 'and these twenty-nine men are twenty-nine of his nobles from Ulster.'

At that news the men of the household picked up clubs and cudgels and every kind of thing that was near, and made a violent and woeful attack on Tibraidè's men. The King of Leinster came in then, and when he was told Tibraidè was Mongan he attacked them as well, and it was with difficulty that Tibraidè got away to Cell Camain with nine of his men and they all wounded.

The King of Leinster came back then.

He went to Duv Laca's room.

'Where is Tibraidè?' said he.

'It wasn't Tibraidè was here,' said the hag who was still sitting on the spike, and was not half dead, 'it was Mongan.'

'Why did you let him near you?' said the king to Duv Laca.

'There is no one has a better right to be near me than Mongan has,' said Duv Laca. 'He is my own husband,' said she.

And then the king cried out in dismay:

'I have beaten Tibraidè's people.'

He rushed from the room.

'Send for Tibraidè till I apologize,' he cried. 'Tell him it was all a mistake. Tell him it was Mongan.'

CHAPTER XVIII

Mongan and his servant went home, and (for what pleasure is greater than that of memory exercised in conversation?) for a time the feeling of an adventure well accomplished kept him in some contentment. But at the end of a time that pleasure was worn out, and Mongan grew at first dispirited and then sullen, and after that as ill as he had been on the previous occasion. For he could not forget Duv Laca of the White Hand, and he could not remember her without longing and despair.

It was in the illness which comes from longing and despair that he sat one day looking on a world that was black although the sun shone, and that was lean and unwholesome although autumn fruits were heavy on the earth and the joys of harvest were about him.

'Winter is in my heart,' quoth he, 'and I am cold already.'

He thought too that some day he would die, and the thought was not unpleasant, for one half of his life was away in the territories of the King of Leinster, and the half that he kept in himself had no spice in it.

He was thinking in this way when mac an Dáv came towards him over the lawn, and he noticed that mac an Dáv was walking like an old man.

He took little slow steps, and he did not loosen his knees when he walked, so he went stiffly. One of his feet turned pitifully outwards, and the other turned lamentably in. His chest was pulled inwards, and his head was stuck outwards and hung down in the place where his chest should have been, and his arms were crooked in front of him with the hands turned wrongly, so that one palm was shown to the east of the world and the other one was turned to the west.

'How goes it, mac an Dáv?' said the king.

'Bad,' said mac an Dáv.

'Is that the sun I see shining, my friend?' the king asked.

'It may be the sun,' replied mac an Dáv, peering curiously at the golden radiance that dozed about them, 'but maybe it's a yellow fog.'

'What is life at all?' said the king.

'It is a weariness and a tiredness,' said mac an Dáv. 'It is a long yawn without sleepiness. It is a bee, lost at midnight and buzzing on a pane. It is the noise made by a tied-up dog. It is nothing worth dreaming about. It is nothing at all.'

'How well you explain my feelings about Duv Laca,' said the king.

'I was thinking about my own lamb,' said mac an Dáv. 'I was thinking about my own treasure, my cup of cheeriness, and the pulse of my heart.' And with that he burst into tears.

'Alas!' said the king.

'But,' sobbed mac an Dáv, 'what right have I to complain? I am only the servant, and although I didn't make any bargain with the King of Leinster or with any king of them all, yet my wife is gone away as if she was the consort of a potentate the same as Duv Laca is.'

Mongan was sorry then for his servant, and he roused himself.

'I am going to send you to Duv Laca.'

'Where the one is the other will be,' cried mac an Dáv joyously.

'Go,' said Mongan, 'to Rath Descirt of Bregia; you know that place?'

'As well as my tongue knows my teeth.'

'Duv Laca is there; see her, and ask her what she wants me to do.'

Mac an Dáv went there and returned.

'Duv Laca says that you are to come at once, for the King of Leinster is journeying around his territory, and Kevin Cochlach, the charioteer, is making bitter love to her and wants her to run away with him.'

Mongan set out, and in no great time, for they travelled day and night, they came to Bregia, and gained admittance to the fortress, but just as he got in he had to go out again, for the King of Leinster had been warned of Mongan's journey, and came back to his fortress in the nick of time.

When the men of Ulster saw the condition into which Mongan fell they were in great distress, and they all got sick through compassion for their king. The nobles suggested to him that they should march against Leinster and kill that king and bring back Duv Laca, but Mongan would not consent to this plan.

'For,' said he, 'the thing I lost through my own folly I shall get back through my own craft.'

And when he said that his spirits revived, and he called for mac an Dáv.

'You know, my friend,' said Mongan, 'that I can't get Duv Laca back unless the King of Leinster asks me to take her back, for a bargain is a bargain.'

'That will happen when pigs fly,' said mac an Dáv, 'and,' said he, 'I did not make any bargain with any king that is in the world.'

'I heard you say that before,' said Mongan.

'I will say it till Doom,' cried his servant, 'for my wife has gone away with that pestilent king, and he has got the double of your bad bargain.'

Mongan and his servant then set out for Leinster.

When they neared that country they found a great crowd going on the road with them, and they learned that the king was giving a feast in honour of his marriage to Duv Laca, for the year of waiting was nearly out, and the king had sworn he would delay no longer.

They went on, therefore, but in low spirits, and at last they saw the walls of the king's castle towering before them, and a noble company going to and fro on the lawn.

CHAPTER XIX

They sat in a place where they could watch the castle and compose themselves after their journey.

'How are we going to get into the castle?' asked mac an Dáv.

For there were hatchetmen on guard in the big gateway, and there were spearmen at short intervals around the walls, and men to throw hot porridge off the roof were standing in the right places.

'If we cannot get in by hook, we will get in by crook,' said Mongan.

'They are both good ways,' said mac an Dáv, 'and whichever of them you decide on I'll stick by.'

Just then they saw the Hag of the Mill coming out of the mill which was down the road a little.

Now the Hag of the Mill was a bony, thin pole of a hag with odd feet. That is, she had one foot that was too big for her, so that when she lifted it up it pulled her over; and she had one foot that was too small for her, so that when she lifted it up she didn't know what to do with it. She was so long that you thought you would never see the end of her, and she was so thin that you thought you didn't see her at all. One of her eyes was set where her nose should be and there was an ear in its place, and her nose itself was hanging out of her chin, and she had whiskers round it. She was dressed in a red rag that was really a hole with a fringe on it, and she was singing 'Oh, hush thee, my one love' to a cat that was yelping on her shoulder.

She had a tall skinny dog behind her called Brotar. It hadn't a tooth in its head except one, and it had the toothache in that tooth. Every few steps it used to sit down on its hunkers and point its nose straight upwards, and make a long, sad complaint about its tooth; and after that it used to reach its hind leg round and try to scratch out its tooth; and then it used to be pulled on again by the straw rope that was round its neck, and which was tied at the other end to the hag's heaviest foot.

There was an old, knock-kneed, raw-boned, one-eyed, little-winded, heavy-headed mare with her also. Every time it put a front leg forward it shivered all over the rest of its legs backwards, and when it put a hind leg forward it shivered all over the rest of its legs frontwards, and it used to give a great whistle through its nose when it was out of breath, and a big, thin hen was sitting on its croup.

Mongan looked on the Hag of the Mill with delight and affection.

'This time,' said he to mac an Dáv, 'I'll get back my wife.'

'You will indeed,' said mac an Dáv heartily, 'and you'll get mine back too.'

'Go over yonder,' said Mongan, 'and tell the Hag of the Mill that I want to talk to her.'

Mac an Dáv brought her over to him.

'Is it true what the servant man said?' she asked.

'What did he say?' said Mongan.

'He said you wanted to talk to me.'

'It is true,' said Mongan.

'This is a wonderful hour and a glorious minute,' said the hag, 'for this is the first time in sixty years that any one wanted to talk to me. Talk on now,' said she, 'and I'll listen to you if I can remember how to do it. Talk gently,' said she, 'the way you won't disturb the animals, for they are all sick.'

'They are sick indeed,' said mac an Dáv pityingly.

'The cat has a sore tail,' said she, 'by reason of sitting too close to a part of the hob that was hot. The dog has a toothache, the horse has a pain in her stomach, and the hen has the pip.'

'Ah, it's a sad world,' said mac an Dáv.

'There you are!' said the hag.

'Tell me,' Mongan commenced, 'if you got a wish, what it is you would wish for?'

The hag took the cat off her shoulder and gave it to mac an Dáv.

'Hold that for me while I think,' said she.

'Would you like to be a lovely young girl?' asked Mongan.

'I'd sooner be that than a skinned eel,' said she.

'And would you like to marry me or the King of Leinster?'

'I'd like to marry either of you, or both of you, or whichever of you came first.'

'Very well,' said Mongan, 'you shall have your wish.'

He touched her with his finger, and the instant he touched her all dilapidation and wryness and age went from her, and she became so beautiful that one dared scarcely look on her, and so young that she seemed but sixteen years of age.

'You are not the Hag of the Mill any longer,' said Mongan, 'you are Ivell of the Shining Cheeks, daughter of the King of Munster.'

He touched the dog too, and it became a little silky lapdog that could nestle in your palm. Then he changed the old mare into a brisk piebald palfrey. Then he changed himself so that he became the living image of Ae, the son of the King of Connaught, who had just been married to Ivell of the Shining Cheeks, and then he changed mac an Dáv into the likeness of Ae's attendant, and then they all set off towards the fortress, singing the song that begins:

My wife is nicer than any one's wife,
  Any one's wife, any one's wife,
My wife is nicer than any one's wife,
  Which nobody can deny.

CHAPTER XX

The doorkeeper brought word to the King of Leinster that the son of the King of Connaught, Ae the Beautiful, and his wife, Ivell of the

Shining Cheeks, were at the door, that they had been banished from Connaught by Ae's father, and they were seeking the protection of the King of Leinster.

Branduv came to the door himself to welcome them, and the minute he looked on Ivell of the Shining Cheeks it was plain that he liked looking at her.

It was now drawing towards evening, and a feast was prepared for the guests with a banquet to follow it. At the feast Duv Laca sat beside the King of Leinster, but Mongan sat opposite him with Ivell, and Mongan put more and more magic into the hag, so that her cheeks shone and her eyes gleamed, and she was utterly bewitching to the eye; and when Branduv looked at her she seemed to grow more and more lovely and more and more desirable, and at last there was not a bone in his body as big as an inch that was not filled with love and longing for the girl.

Every few minutes he gave a great sigh as if he had eaten too much, and when Duv Laca asked him if he had eaten too much he said he had but that he had not drunk enough, and by that he meant that he had not drunk enough from the eyes of the girl before him.

At the banquet which was then held he looked at her again, and every time he took a drink he toasted Ivell across the brim of his goblet, and in a little while she began to toast him back across the rim of her cup, for he was drinking ale, but she was drinking mead. Then he sent a messenger to her to say that it was a far better thing to be the wife of the King of Leinster than to be the wife of the son of the King of Connaught, for a king is better than a prince, and Ivell thought that this was as wise a thing as anybody had ever said.

And then he sent a message to say that he loved her so much that he would certainly burst of love if it did not stop.

Mongan heard the whispering, and he told the hag that if she did what he advised she would certainly get either himself or the King of Leinster for a husband.

'Either of you will be welcome,' said the hag.

'When the king says he loves you, ask him to prove it by gifts; ask for his drinking-horn first.'

She asked for that, and he sent it to her filled with good liquor; then she asked for his girdle, and he sent her that.

His people argued with him and said it was not right that he should give away the treasures of Leinster to the wife of the King of Connaught's son; but he said that it did not matter, for when he got the girl he would get his treasures with her. But every time he sent anything to the hag, mac an Dáv snatched it out of her lap and put it in his pocket.

'Now,' said Mongan to the hag, 'tell the servant to say that you would not leave your own husband for all the wealth of the world.'

She told the servant that, and the servant told it to the king.

When Branduv heard it he nearly went mad with love and longing and jealousy, and with rage also, because of the treasure he had given her and might not get back. He called Mongan over to him, and spoke to him very threateningly and ragingly.

'I am not one who takes a thing without giving a thing,' said he.

'Nobody could say you were,' agreed Mongan.

'Do you see this woman sitting beside me?' he continued, pointing to Duv Laca.

'I do indeed,' said Mongan.

'Well,' said Branduv, 'this woman is Duv Laca of the White Hand that I took away from Mongan; she is just going to marry me, but if you will make an exchange, you can marry this Duv Laca here, and I will marry that Ivell of the Shining Cheeks yonder.'

Mongan pretended to be very angry then.

'If I had come here with horses and treasure you would be in your right to take these from me, but you have no right to ask for what you are now asking.'

'I do ask for it,' said Branduv menacingly, 'and you must not refuse a lord.'

'Very well,' said Mongan reluctantly, and as if in great fear; 'if you will make the exchange I will make it, although it breaks my heart.'

He brought Ivell over to the king then and gave her three kisses.

'The king would suspect something if I did not kiss you,' said he, and then he gave the hag over to the king.

After that they all got drunk and merry, and soon there was a great snoring and snorting, and very soon all the servants fell asleep also, so that Mongan could not get anything to drink. Mac an Dáv said it was a great shame, and he kicked some of the servants, but they did not budge, and then he slipped out to the stables and saddled two mares. He got on one with his wife behind him and Mongan got on the other with Duv Laca behind him, and they rode away towards Ulster like the wind, singing this song:

The King of Leinster was married to-day.
  Married to-day, married to-day.
The King of Leinster was married to-day,
  And every one wishes him joy.

In the morning the servants came to waken the King of Leinster, and when they saw the face of the hag lying on the pillow beside the king, and her nose all covered with whiskers, and her big foot and little foot sticking away out at the end of the bed, they began to laugh, and poke one another in the stomach and thump one another on the shoulder, so that the noise awakened the king, and he asked what was the matter with them at all. It was then he saw the hag lying beside him, and he gave a great screech and jumped out of the bed.

'Aren't you the Hag of the Mill?' said he.

'I am indeed,' she replied, 'and I love you dearly.'

'I wish I didn't see you,' said Branduv.

That was the end of the story, and when he had told it Mongan began to laugh uproariously and called for more wine. He drank this deeply, as though he was full of thirst and despair and a wild jollity, but when the Flame Lady began to weep he took her in his arms and caressed her, and said that she was the love of his heart and the one treasure of the world.

After that they feasted in great contentment, and at the end of the feasting they went away from Faery and returned to the world of men.

They came to Mongan's palace at Moy Linney, and it was not until they reached the palace that they found they had been away one whole year, for they had thought they were only away one night. They lived then peacefully and lovingly together, and that ends the story, but Brótiarna did not know that Mongan was Fionn.

The abbot leaned forward.

'Was Mongan Fionn?' he asked in a whisper.

'He was,' replied Cairidè.

'Indeed, indeed!' said the abbot.

After a while he continued. 'There is only one part of your story that I do not like.'

'What part is that?' asked Cairidè.

'It is the part where the holy man Tibraidè was ill-treated by that rap – by that – by Mongan.'

Cairidè agreed that it was ill done, but to himself he said gleefully that whenever he was asked to tell the story of how he told the story of Mongan he would remember what the abbot said.

THE STORY OF
TUAN MAC CAIRILL

By James Stephens

CHAPTER I

Finnian, the Abbot of Moville, went southwards and eastwards in great haste. News had come to him in Donegal that there were yet people in his own province who believed in gods that he did not approve of, and the gods that we do not approve of are treated scurvily, even by saintly men.

He was told of a powerful gentleman who observed neither Saint's day nor Sunday.

'A powerful person!' said Finnian.

'All that,' was the reply.

'We shall try this person's power,' said Finnian.

'He is reputed to be a wise and hardy man,' said his informant.

'We shall test his wisdom and his hardihood.'

'He is,' that gossip whispered – 'he is a magician.'

'I will magician him,' cried Finnian angrily. 'Where does that man live?'

He was informed, and he proceeded in that direction without delay.

In no great time he came to the stronghold of the gentleman who followed ancient ways, and he demanded admittance in order that he might preach and prove the new God, and exorcize and terrify and banish even the memory of the old one; for to a god grown old Time is as ruthless as to a beggarman grown old.

But the Ulster gentleman refused Finnian admittance.

He barricaded his house, he shuttered his windows, and in a gloom of indignation and protest he continued the practices of ten thousand years, and would not hearken to Finnian calling at the window or to Time knocking at his door.

But of those adversaries it was the first he redoubted.

Finnian loomed on him as a portent and a terror; but he had no fear of Time. Indeed he was the foster-brother of Time, and so disdainful of the bitter god that he did not even disdain him; he leaped over the scythe, he dodged under it, and the sole occasions on which Time laughs is when he chances on Tuan, the son of Cairill, the son of Muredac Red-neck.

CHAPTER II

Now Finnian could not abide that any person should resist both the Gospel and himself, and he proceeded to force the stronghold by peaceful but powerful methods. He fasted on the gentleman, and he did so to such purpose that he was admitted to the house; for to an hospitable heart the idea that a stranger may expire on your doorstep from sheer famine cannot be tolerated. The gentleman, however, did not give in without a struggle: he thought that when Finnian had grown sufficiently hungry he would lift the siege and take himself off to some place where he might get food. But he did not know Finnian. The great abbot sat down on a spot just beyond the door, and composed himself to all that might follow from his action. He bent his gaze on the ground between his feet, and entered into a meditation from which he would only be released by admission or death.

The first day passed quietly.

Often the gentleman would send a servitor to spy if that deserter of the gods was still before his door, and each time the servant replied that he was still there.

'He will be gone in the morning,' said the hopeful master.

On the morrow the state of siege continued, and through that day the servants were sent many times to observe through spy-holes.

'Go,' he would say, 'and find out if the worshipper of new gods has taken himself away.'

But the servants returned each time with the same information.

'The new druid is still there,' they said.

All through that day no one could leave the stronghold. And the enforced seclusion wrought on the minds of the servants, while the cessation of all work banded them together in small groups that whispered and discussed and disputed. Then these groups would disperse to peep through the spy-hole at the patient immobile figure seated before the door, wrapped in a meditation that was timeless and unconcerned. They took fright at the spectacle, and once or twice a woman screamed hysterically, and was bundled away with a companion's hand clapped on her mouth, so that the ear of their master should not be affronted.

'He has his own troubles,' they said. 'It is a combat of the gods that is taking place.'

So much for the women; but the men also were uneasy. They prowled up and down, tramping from the spy-hole to the kitchen, and from the kitchen to the turreted roof. And from the roof they would look down on the motionless figure below, and speculate on many things, including the staunchness of man, the qualities of their master, and even the possibility that the new gods might be as powerful as the old. From these peepings and discussions they would return languid and discouraged.

'If,' said one irritable guard, 'if we buzzed a spear at that persistent stranger, or if one slung at him with a jagged pebble!'

'What!' his master demanded wrathfully, 'is a spear to be thrown at an unarmed stranger? And from this house!'

And he soundly cuffed that indelicate servant.

'Be at peace all of you,' he said, 'for hunger has a whip, and he will drive the stranger away in the night.'

The household retired to wretched beds; but for the master of the house there was no sleep. He marched his halls all night, going often to the spy-hole to see if that shadow was still sitting in the shade, and pacing thence, tormented, preoccupied, refusing even the nose of his favourite dog as it pressed lovingly into his closed palm.

On the morrow he gave in.

The great door was swung wide, and two of his servants carried Finnian into the house, for the saint could no longer walk or stand

upright by reason of the hunger and exposure to which he had submitted. But his frame was tough as the unconquerable spirit that dwelt within it, and in no long time he was ready for whatever might come of dispute or anathema.

Being quite re-established he undertook the conversion of the master of the house, and the siege he laid against that notable intelligence was long spoken of among those who are interested in such things.

He had beaten the disease of Mugain; he had beaten his own pupil the great Colm Cillé; he beat Tuan also, and just as the latter's door had opened to the persistent stranger, so his heart opened, and Finnian marched there to do the will of God, and his own will.

CHAPTER III

One day they were talking together about the majesty of God and His love, for although Tuan had now received much instruction on this subject he yet needed more, and he laid as close a siege on Finnian as Finnian had before that laid on him. But man works outwardly and inwardly, after rest he has energy, after energy he needs repose; so, when we have given instruction for a time, we need instruction, and must receive it or the spirit faints and wisdom herself grows bitter.

Therefore Finnian said: 'Tell me now about yourself, dear heart.'

But Tuan was avid of information about the True God.

'No, no,' he said, 'the past has nothing more of interest for me, and I do not wish anything to come between my soul and its instruction; continue to teach me, dear friend and saintly father.'

'I will do that,' Finnian replied, 'but I must first meditate deeply on you, and must know you well. Tell me your past, my beloved, for a man is his past, and is to be known by it.'

But Tuan pleaded:

'Let the past be content with itself, for man needs forgetfulness as well as memory.'

'My son,' said Finnian, 'all that has ever been done has been done for the glory of God, and to confess our good and evil deeds is part of instruction; for the soul must recall its acts and abide by them, or renounce them by confession and penitence. Tell me your genealogy first, and by what descent you occupy these lands and stronghold, and then I will examine your acts and your conscience.'

Tuan replied obediently:

'I am known as Tuan, son of Cairill, son of Muredac Red-neck, and these are the hereditary lands of my father.'

The saint nodded.

'I am not as well acquainted with Ulster genealogies as I should be, yet I know something of them. I am by blood a Leinsterman,' he continued.

'Mine is a long pedigree,' Tuan murmured.

Finnian received that information with respect and interest.

'I also,' he said, 'have an honourable record.'

His host continued:

'I am indeed Tuan, the son of Starn, the son of Sera, who was brother to Partholon.'

'But,' said Finnian in bewilderment, 'there is an error here, for you have recited two different genealogies.'

'Different genealogies, indeed,' replied Tuan thoughtfully, 'but they are my genealogies.'

'I do not understand this,' Finnian declared roundly.

'I am now known as Tuan mac Cairill,' the other replied, 'but in the days of old I was known as Tuan mac Starn, mac Sera.'

'The brother of Partholon,' the saint gasped.

'That is my pedigree,' Tuan said.

'But,' Finnian objected in bewilderment, 'Partholon came to Ireland not long after the Flood.'

'I came with him,' said Tuan mildly.

The saint pushed his chair back hastily, and sat staring at his host, and as he stared the blood grew chill in his veins, and his hair crept along his scalp and stood on end.

CHAPTER IV

But Finnian was not one who remained long in bewilderment. He thought on the might of God and he became that might, and was tranquil.

He was one who loved God and Ireland, and to the person who could instruct him in these great themes he gave all the interest of his mind and the sympathy of his heart.

'It is a wonder you tell me, my beloved,' he said. 'And now you must tell me more.'

'What must I tell?' asked Tuan resignedly.

'Tell me of the beginning of time in Ireland, and of the bearing of Partholon, the son of Noah's son.'

'I have almost forgotten him,' said Tuan. 'A greatly bearded, greatly shouldered man he was. A man of sweet deeds and sweet ways.'

'Continue, my love,' said Finnian.

'He came to Ireland in a ship. Twenty-four men and twenty-four women came with him. But before that time no man had come to Ireland, and in the western parts of the world no human being lived or moved. As we drew on Ireland from the sea the country seemed like an unending forest. Far as the eye could reach, and in whatever direction, there were trees; and from these there came the unceasing singing of birds. Over all that land the sun shone warm and beautiful, so that to our sea-weary eyes, our wind-tormented ears, it seemed as if we were driving on Paradise.

'We landed and we heard the rumble of water going gloomily through the darkness of the forest. Following the water we came to a glade where the sun shone and where the earth was warmed, and there Partholon rested with his twenty-four couples, and made a city and a livelihood.

'There were fish in the rivers of Éire, there were animals in her coverts. Wild and shy and monstrous creatures ranged in her plains and forests. Creatures that one could see through and walk through. Long we lived in ease, and we saw new animals grow – the bear, the wolf, the badger, the deer, and the boar.

'Partholon's people increased until from twenty-four couples there came five thousand people, who lived in amity and contentment although they had no wits.'

'They had no wits!' Finnian commented.

'They had no need of wits,' Tuan said.

'I have heard that the first-born were mindless,' said Finnian. 'Continue your story, my beloved.'

'Then, sudden as a rising wind, between one night and a morning, there came a sickness that bloated the stomach and purpled the skin,

and on the seventh day all of the race of Partholon were dead, save one man only.'

'There always escapes one man,' said Finnian thoughtfully.

'And I am that man,' his companion affirmed.

Tuan shaded his brow with his hand, and he remembered backwards through incredible ages to the beginning of the world and the first days of Éire. And Finnian, with his blood again running chill and his scalp crawling uneasily, stared backwards with him.

CHAPTER V

'Tell on, my love,' Finnian murmured.

'I was alone,' said Tuan. 'I was so alone that my own shadow frightened me. I was so alone that the sound of a bird in flight, or the creaking of a dew-drenched bough whipped me to cover as a rabbit is scared to his burrow.

'The creatures of the forest scented me and knew I was alone. They stole with silken pad behind my back and snarled when I faced them; the long, grey wolves with hanging tongues and staring eyes chased me to my cleft rock; there was no creature so weak but it might hunt me; there was no creature so timid but it might outface me. And so I lived for two tens of years and two years, until I knew all that a beast surmises and had forgotten all that a man had known.

'I could pad as gently as any; I could run as tirelessly. I could be invisible and patient as a wild cat crouching among leaves; I could smell danger in my sleep and leap at it with wakeful claws; I could bark and growl and clash with my teeth and tear with them.'

'Tell on, my beloved,' said Finnian; 'you shall rest in God, dear heart.'

'At the end of that time,' said Tuan, 'Nemed the son of Agnoman came to Ireland with a fleet of thirty-four barques, and in each barque there were thirty couples of people.'

'I have heard it,' said Finnian.

'My heart leaped for joy when I saw the great fleet rounding the land, and I followed them along scarped cliffs, leaping from rock to rock like a wild goat, while the ships tacked and swung seeking a harbour. There I stooped to drink at a pool, and I saw myself in the chill water.

'I saw that I was hairy and tufty and bristled as a savage boar; that I was lean as a stripped bush; that I was greyer than a badger; withered and wrinkled like an empty sack; naked as a fish; wretched as a starving crow in winter; and on my fingers and toes there were great curving claws, so that I looked like nothing that was known, like nothing that was animal or divine. And I sat by the pool weeping my loneliness and wildness and my stern old age; and I could do no more than cry and lament between the earth and the sky, while the beasts that tracked me listened from behind the trees, or crouched among bushes to stare at me from their drowsy covert.

'A storm arose, and when I looked again from my tall cliff I saw that great fleet rolling as in a giant's hand. At times they were pitched against the sky and staggered aloft, spinning gustily there like wind-blown leaves. Then they were hurled from these dizzy tops to the flat, moaning gulf, to the glassy, inky horror that swirled and whirled between ten waves. At times a wave leaped howling under a ship, and with a buffet dashed it into air, and chased it upwards with thunder stroke on stroke, and followed again, close as

a chasing wolf, trying with hammering on hammering to beat in the wide-wombed bottom and suck out the frightened lives through one black gape. A wave fell on a ship and sank it down with a thrust, stern as though a whole sky had tumbled at it, and the barque did not cease to go down until it crashed and sank in the sand at the bottom of the sea.

'The night came, and with it a thousand darknesses fell from the screeching sky. Not a round-eyed creature of the night might pierce an inch of that multiplied gloom. Not a creature dared creep or stand. For a great wind strode the world lashing its league-long whips in cracks of thunder, and singing to itself, now in a world-wide yell, now in an ear-dizzying hum and buzz; or with a long snarl and whine it hovered over the world searching for life to destroy.

'And at times, from the moaning and yelping blackness of the sea, there came a sound – thin-drawn as from millions of miles away, distinct as though uttered in the ear like a whisper of confidence – and I knew that a drowning man was calling on his God as he thrashed and was battered into silence, and that a blue-lipped woman was calling on her man as her hair whipped round her brows and she whirled about like a top.

'Around me the trees were dragged from earth with dying groans; they leaped into the air and flew like birds. Great waves whizzed from the sea: spinning across the cliffs and hurtling to the earth in monstrous clots of foam; the very rocks came trundling and sidling and grinding among the trees; and in that rage, and in that horror of blackness, I fell asleep, or I was beaten into slumber.'

CHAPTER VI

'There I dreamed, and I saw myself changing into a stag in dream, and I felt in dream the beating of a new heart within me, and in dream I arched my neck and braced my powerful limbs.

'I awoke from the dream, and I was that which I had dreamed.

'I stood a while stamping upon a rock, with my bristling head swung high, breathing through wide nostrils all the savour of the world. For I had come marvellously from decrepitude to strength. I had writhed from the bonds of age and was young again. I smelled the turf and knew for the first time how sweet that smelled. And like lightning my moving nose sniffed all things to my heart and separated them into knowledge.

'Long I stood there, ringing my iron hoof on stone, and learning all things through my nose. Each breeze that came from the right hand or the left brought me a tale. A wind carried me the tang of wolf, and against that smell I stared and stamped. And on a wind there came the scent of my own kind, and at that I belled. Oh, loud and clear and sweet was the voice of the great stag. With what ease my lovely note went lilting. With what joy I heard the answering call. With what delight I bounded, bounded, bounded; light as a bird's plume, powerful as a storm, untiring as the sea.

'Here now was ease in ten-yard springings, with a swinging head, with the rise and fall of a swallow, with the curve and flow and urge of an otter of the sea. What a tingle dwelt about my heart! What a thrill spun to the lofty points of my antlers! How the world was new! How the sun was new! How the wind caressed me!

'With unswerving forehead and steady eye I met all that came. The old, lone wolf leaped sideways, snarling, and slunk away. The lumbering bear swung his head of hesitations and thought again; he trotted his small red eye away with him to a near-by brake. The stags of my race fled from my rocky forehead, or were pushed back and back until their legs broke under them and I trampled them to death. I was the beloved, the well known, the leader of the herds of Ireland.

'And at times I came back from my boundings about Éire, for the strings of my heart were drawn to Ulster; and, standing away, my wide nose took the air, while I knew with joy, with terror, that men were blown on the wind. A proud head hung to the turf then, and the tears of memory rolled from a large, bright eye.

'At times I drew near, delicately, standing among thick leaves or crouched in long grown grasses, and I stared and mourned as I looked on men. For Nemed and four couples had been saved from that fierce storm, and I saw them increase and multiply until four thousand couples lived and laughed and were riotous in the sun, for the people of Nemed had small minds but great activity. They were savage fighters and hunters.

'But one time I came, drawn by that intolerable anguish of memory, and all of these people were gone: the place that knew them was silent: in the land where they had moved there was nothing of them but their bones that glinted in the sun.

'Old age came on me there. Among these bones weariness crept into my limbs. My head grew heavy, my eyes dim, my knees jerked and trembled, and there the wolves dared chase me.

'I went again to the cave that had been my home when I was an old man.

'One day I stole from the cave to snatch a mouthful of grass, for I was closely besieged by wolves. They made their rush, and I barely escaped from them. They sat beyond the cave staring at me.

'I knew their tongue. I knew all that they said to each other, and all that they said to me. But there was yet a thud left in my forehead, a deadly trample in my hoof. They did not dare come into the cave.

'"Tomorrow," they said, "we will tear out your throat, and gnaw on your living haunch."'

CHAPTER VII

'Then my soul rose to the height of Doom, and I intended all that might happen to me, and agreed to it.

'"To-morrow," I said, "I will go out among ye, and I will die," and at that the wolves howled joyfully, hungrily, impatiently.

'I slept, and I saw myself changing into a boar in dream, and I felt in dream the beating of a new heart within me, and in dream I stretched my powerful neck and braced my eager limbs. I awoke from my dream, and I was that which I had dreamed.

'The night wore away, the darkness lifted, the day came; and from without the cave the wolves called to me:

'"Come out, O Skinny Stag. Come out and die."

'And I, with joyful heart, thrust a black bristle through the hole of the cave, and when they saw that wriggling snout, those curving tusks, that red fierce eye, the wolves fled yelping, tumbling over each other, frantic with terror; and I behind them, a wild-cat for leaping, a giant for strength, a devil for ferocity; a madness and gladness of lusty unsparing life; a killer, a champion, a boar who could not be defied.

'I took the lordship of the boars of Ireland.

'Wherever I looked among my tribes I saw love and obedience: whenever I appeared among the strangers they fled away. Ah, the wolves feared me then, and the great, grim bear went bounding on heavy paws. I charged him at the head of my troop and rolled him over and over; but it is not easy to kill the bear, so deeply is his life packed under that stinking pelt. He picked himself up and ran, and was knocked down, and ran again blindly, butting into trees and stones. Not a claw did the big bear flash, not a tooth did he show, as he ran whimpering like a baby, or as he stood with my nose rammed against his mouth, snarling up into his nostrils.

'I challenged all that moved. All creatures but one. For men had again come to Ireland. Semion, the son of Stariath, with his people, from whom the men of Domnann and the Fir Bolg and the Galiuin are descended. These I did not chase, and when they chased me I fled.

'Often I would go, drawn by my memoried heart, to look at them as they moved among their fields; and I spoke to my mind in bitterness:

'When the people of Partholon were gathered in counsel my voice was heard; it was sweet to all who heard it, and the words I spoke were wise. The eyes of women brightened and softened when they looked at me. They loved to hear him when he sang who now wanders in the forest with a tusky herd.'

CHAPTER VIII

'Old age again overtook me. Weariness stole into my limbs, and anguish dozed into my mind. I went to my Ulster cave and dreamed my dream, and I changed into a hawk.

'I left the ground. The sweet air was my kingdom, and my bright eye stared on a hundred miles. I soared, I swooped; I hung, motionless as a living stone, over the abyss; I lived in joy and slept in peace, and had my fill of the sweetness of life.

'During that time Beothach, the son of Iarbonel the Prophet, came to Ireland with his people, and there was a great battle between his men and the children of Semion. Long I hung over that combat, seeing every spear that hurtled, every stone that whizzed from a sling, every sword that flashed up and down, and the endless glittering of the shields. And at the end I saw that the victory was with Iarbonel. And from his people the Tuatha Dè and the Andè came, although their origin is forgotten, and learned people, because of their excellent wisdom and intelligence, say that they came from heaven.

'These are the people of Faery. All these are the gods.

'For long, long years I was a hawk. I knew every hill and stream; every field and glen of Ireland. I knew the shape of cliffs and coasts, and how all places looked under the sun or moon. And I was still a hawk when the sons of Mil drove the Tuatha Dè Danann under the ground, and held Ireland against arms or wizardry; and this was the coming of men and the beginning of genealogics.

'Then I grew old, and in my Ulster cave close to the sea I dreamed my dream, and in it I became a salmon. The green tides of Ocean rose over me and my dream, so that I drowned in the sea and did not die, for I awoke in deep waters, and I was that which I dreamed.

'I had been a man, a stag, a boar, a bird, and now I was a fish. In all my changes I had joy and fullness of life. But in the water joy lay deeper, life pulsed deeper. For on land or air there is always something excessive and hindering; as arms that swing at the sides

of a man, and which the mind must remember. The stag has legs to be tucked away for sleep, and untucked for movement; and the bird has wings that must be folded and pecked and cared for. But the fish has but one piece from his nose to his tail. He is complete, single and unencumbered. He turns in one turn, and goes up and down and round in one sole movement.

'How I flew through the soft element: how I joyed in the country where there is no harshness: in the element which upholds and gives way; which caresses and lets go, and will not let you fall. For man may stumble in a furrow; the stag tumble from a cliff; the hawk, wing-weary and beaten, with darkness around him and the storm behind, may dash his brains against a tree. But the home of the salmon is his delight, and the sea guards all her creatures.'

CHAPTER IX

'I became the king of the salmon, and, with my multitudes, I ranged on the tides of the world. Green and purple distances were under me: green and gold the sunlit regions above. In these latitudes I moved through a world of amber, myself amber and gold; in those others, in a sparkle of lucent blue, I curved, lit like a living jewel: and in these again, through dusks of ebony all mazed with silver, I shot and shone, the wonder of the sea.

'I saw the monsters of the uttermost ocean go heaving by; and the long lithe brutes that are toothed to their tails: and below, where gloom dipped down on gloom, vast, livid tangles that coiled and uncoiled, and lapsed down steeps and hells of the sea where even the salmon could not go.

'I knew the sea. I knew the secret caves where ocean roars to ocean; the floods that are icy cold, from which the nose of a salmon leaps back as at a sting; and the warm streams in which we rocked and dozed and were carried forward without motion. I swam on the outermost rim of the great world, where nothing was but the sea and the sky and the salmon; where even the wind was silent, and the water was clear as clean grey rock.

'And then, far away in the sea, I remembered Ulster, and there came on me an instant, uncontrollable anguish to be there. I turned, and through days and nights I swam tirelessly, jubilantly; with terror wakening in me, too, and a whisper through my being that I must reach Ireland or die.

'I fought my way to Ulster from the sea.

'Ah, how that end of the journey was hard! A sickness was racking in every one of my bones, a languor and weariness creeping through my every fibre and muscle. The waves held me back and held me back; the soft waters seemed to have grown hard; and it was as though I were urging through a rock as I strained towards Ulster from the sea.

'So tired I was! I could have loosened my frame and been swept away; I could have slept and been drifted and wafted away; swinging on grey-green billows that had turned from the land and were heaving and mounting and surging to the far blue water.

'Only the unconquerable heart of the salmon could brave that end of toil. The sound of the rivers of Ireland racing down to the sea came to me in the last numb effort: the love of Ireland bore me up: the gods of the rivers trod to me in the white-curled breakers, so that I left the sea at long, long last; and I lay in sweet water in the curve of a crannied rock, exhausted, three parts dead, triumphant.'

CHAPTER X

'Delight and strength came to me again, and now I explored all the inland ways, the great lakes of Ireland, and her swift brown rivers.

'What a joy to lie under an inch of water basking in the sun, or beneath a shady ledge to watch the small creatures that speed like lightning on the rippling top. I saw the dragon-flies flash and dart and turn, with a poise, with a speed that no other winged thing knows: I saw the hawk hover and stare and swoop: he fell like a falling stone, but he could not catch the king of the salmon: I saw the cold-eyed cat stretching along a bough level with the water, eager to hook and lift the creatures of the river. And I saw men.

'They saw me also. They came to know me and look for me. They lay in wait at the waterfalls up which I leaped like a silver flash. They held out nets for me; they hid traps under leaves; they made cords of the colour of water, of the colour of weeds – but this salmon had a nose that knew how a weed felt and how a string – they drifted meat on a sightless string, but I knew of the hook; they thrust spears at me, and threw lances which they drew back again with a cord.

'Many a wound I got from men, many a sorrowful scar.

'Every beast pursued me in the waters and along the banks; the barking, black-skinned otter came after me in lust and gust and swirl; the wild-cat fished for me; the hawk and the steep-winged, spear-beaked birds dived down on me, and men crept on me with nets the width of a river, so that I got no rest. My life became a ceaseless scurry and wound and escape, a burden and anguish of watchfulness – and then I was caught.'

CHAPTER XI

'The fisherman of Cairill, the King of Ulster, took me in his net. Ah, that was a happy man when he saw me! He shouted for joy when he saw the great salmon in his net.

'I was still in the water as he hauled delicately. I was still in the water as he pulled me to the bank. My nose touched air and spun from it as from fire, and I dived with all my might against the bottom of the net, holding yet to the water, loving it, mad with terror that I must quit that loveliness. But the net held and I came up.

'"Be quiet, King of the River," said the fisherman, "give in to Doom," said he.

'I was in air, and it was as though I were in fire. The air pressed on me like a fiery mountain. It beat on my scales and scorched them. It rushed down my throat and scalded me. It weighed on me and squeezed me, so that my eyes felt as though they must burst from my head, my head as though it would leap from my body, and my body as though it would swell and expand and fly in a thousand pieces.

'The light blinded me, the heat tormented me, the dry air made me shrivel and gasp; and, as he lay on the grass the great salmon whirled his desperate nose once more to the river, and leaped, leaped, leaped, even under the mountain of air. He could leap upwards, but not forwards, and yet he leaped, for in each rise he could see the twinkling waves, the rippling and curling waters.

'"Be at ease, O King," said the fisherman. "Be at rest, my beloved. Let go the stream. Let the oozy marge be forgotten, and the sandy bed where the shades dance all in green and gloom, and the brown flood sings along."

'And as he carried me to the palace he sang a song of the river, and a song of Doom, and a song in praise of the King of the Waters.

'When the king's wife saw me she desired me. I was put over a fire and roasted, and she ate me. And when time passed she gave birth to me, and I was her son and the son of Cairill the king. I remember warmth and darkness and movement and unseen sounds. All that happened I remember, from the time I was on the gridiron until the time I was born. I forget nothing of these things.'

'And now,' said Finnian, 'you will be born again, for I shall baptize you into the family of the Living God.'

So far the story of Tuan the son of Cairill.

No man knows if he died in those distant ages when Finnian was Abbot of Moville, or if he still keeps his fort in Ulster, watching all things, and remembering them for the glory of God and the honour of Ireland.